MI

Centenary Collection

Celebrating 100 years of romance with the very best of Mills & Boon

First published in Great Britain 2008
by Harlequin Mills & Boon Limited,
Eton House, 18-24 Paradise Road, Richmond, Surrey TW9 1SR

© Caroline Anderson 2001

ISBN: 978 0 263 86645 2

77-0608

Harlequin Mills & Boon policy is to use papers that are
natural, renewable and recyclable products and made from
wood grown in sustainable forests. The logging and
manufacturing processes conform to the legal environmental
regulations of the country of origin.

Printed and bound in Spain
by Litografía Rosés S.A., Barcelona

A Special Kind of Woman

by

Caroline Anderson

MILLS & BOON

Pure reading pleasure

Caroline Anderson has the mind of a butterfly. She's been a nurse, a secretary, a teacher, run her own soft-furnishing business and now she's settled on writing. She says, 'I was looking for that elusive something. I finally realised it was variety and now I have it in abundance. Every book brings new horizons and new friends, and in between books I have learned to be a juggler. My teacher husband John and I have two beautiful and talented daughters, Sarah and Hannah, umpteen pets and several acres of Suffolk that nature tries to reclaim every time we turn our backs!' Caroline writes for the Mills & Boon® Romance and the Mills & Boon® Medical™ series. Make sure you look out for her latest books!

CHAPTER ONE

'THAT'S it, there.'

Cait looked up at the grim and forbidding exterior of the halls of residence and her heart sank. Oh, lord. Her baby was going to be living here in this dismal grey pile, hemmed in by endless buildings and concrete and dirt and vice—

'Look, Mum, there's a parking place, by that Mercedes.'

So there was. What an unfortunate contrast. She zipped her modest old banger across the road into the space just ahead of another car, triggering a blast on the horn and wild gestures the meaning of which she could only guess at.

She resisted the urge to gesture back, and reversed neatly into place behind the Mercedes. 'OK. I wonder if we've got enough money to feed the meter and keep it quiet for an hour or so?'

'It won't take that long,' Milly said naïvely. 'I've only got a few things.'

Cait glanced in the rear-view mirror at the teetering pile of essentials Milly had simply *had* to bring with her, and sighed. A few things? In her dreams.

She fed the meter—copiously—and then they had to

run the gauntlet of the security system to gain access to the entrance hall. Milly went up to the porter behind his desk in the porter's lodge and smiled a little uncertainly. 'Hi. I'm Emily Cooper. I've got a room here this year?'

'Sure. Cooper—here it is. Here's your swipe card, your room key, information about the phone system, rules of the hall…'

He handed over a sheaf of papers, rattled off some instructions and dropped the key in Milly's outstretched hand. 'Give me a shout if you need any help.'

'Right, let's go and have a look,' Cait said. 'We'll bring in your things in a minute.' She summoned up an encouraging smile, and Milly smiled back, her face a little tight and pale.

To be fair, it was probably pale because of all the wild partying and farewells that had been going on for the past few days, but Cait knew she was also apprehensive.

It was a huge step in her life, and one Cait had no personal experience of to fall back on in her encouragement. She couldn't give her the 'don't do this and you'll enjoy that and try the other' sort of talk she might have been able to under other circumstances, because she'd never made it to university, despite her ambition to read Law. Instead she'd been struggling to raise Emily and keep a roof over their heads.

Not that she'd ever been as clever as her brilliant and multi-talented daughter. Still, she'd done her best for her, kept her nose to the grindstone and been there for her for the last eighteen years.

And now it was time to let go.

Oh, help.

'It looks quite decent,' Milly said slowly, as if she was trying to convince herself. 'At least the paint's new.'

On old and crumbling walls, Cait thought with a

return of her maternal panic. Oh, yipes. She dredged up a smile. 'Here's your room! Look, it's handy for the kitchen. That'll be nice.'

'Not when everyone's making tea in the middle of the night,' Milly said pragmatically and shoved her key in the lock.

The door swung open to reveal a fairly small and barren room. Although like the corridor outside it had been recently decorated, still it seemed bare and forbidding, and Cait's heart sank. There was a bed, a chair, a battered old desk with some wonky shelves over it, a wardrobe in the corner and that was it. Home from home it was not, even though their home was far from luxurious. Poor baby.

'Well, at least it's clean, and the carpet's new, by the look of it,' she said with false cheer. 'What's the bed like?'

Milly bounced experimentally. 'OK. Bit soft.' She stood up and looked out of the window into an inner courtyard, and her face fell. What a dismal view, Cait thought. The bins. Oh, lord.

'At least you won't have the traffic noise from the street,' she said bracingly, and Milly made a small noise that might have been agreement. 'Come on, let's get your things and you can unpack and put everything out on the shelves. It'll look a lot better then.'

Milly made the same noncommittal noise, and with an inward sigh Cait followed her back out to the car. They brought in the cases first, bumping and banging on their legs and the walls of the corridor, and as they struggled up the stairs to the second floor, they had to pause to let two people pass.

The man went first, tall and rugged, flashing her a brief, impersonal smile of thanks that for some reason made her heart beat faster, then a young man Cait thought was probably his son paused beside Emily.

'Hey—Milly, isn't it?' he said, and Milly flipped her hair out of her eyes.

'Hi, Josh!' she exclaimed, and smiled up at him with every appearance of delight. 'What are you doing here?'

'Same as you, I guess.' He lounged against the stair-well wall and grinned. 'So, did you make it to medicine?'

'Yes—did you?'

'Yeah—hey, that's really cool!' His grin widened, and Milly's smile lit up her face.

She's really beautiful, Cait thought with a lump in her throat. Oh, heck. Will she be all right?

'Josh?'

The voice echoed back up the corridor, and he pulled a face. 'Coming!' he called, and flashed her another grin. 'I'll see you around, Milly.' He bounded down the stairs two at a time and disappeared round the corner.

Cait watched him go, tall and gangly but with a cheerful friendliness about him that lightened her spirits. 'So who was that?' she asked Milly casually.

'Oh, his name's Josh something—can't remember. He was at one of the other schools in town—I've seen him around. He went out with Jo for a bit. I met him on a conference in Cambridge as well, but I haven't seen him for ages.'

'Well, it's someone you know, anyway,' Cait said, relieved as much for herself as for her daughter. 'It's always nice to see a familiar face, and he seemed pleased to see you. Come on, let's get these bags in.'

The bags were the easy bit. The boxes were much more of a challenge, and Cait was wondering how on earth she was going to get up the stairs with the last one, a hugely awkward lump that seemed determined to defeat her, when she felt the weight taken out of her hands.

'Here, let me,' a soft, deep voice murmured.

'Thanks.' She stepped back and smiled, then their eyes met and her heart hiccuped behind her ribs. 'Oh— you're Josh's father,' she said inanely.

'That's right. Owen Douglas.'

'I'm Milly's mother—Cait Cooper.'

'Her *mother*? Good heavens. I thought you were her sister or aunt or something.'

Flattery? If it weren't for the wedding ring on his hand and the fact that *he* was helping *her*, not the other way round, she would have thought he wanted something. Under the circumstances she gave him the benefit of the doubt and blamed it on the poor lighting.

'Hardly,' she said, studying him and thinking what a terrible shame it was that he was married. Not that he'd be interested in her. No man worth having ever was. Oh, well.

He flashed her a rueful smile over the top of the box that nearly melted the soles of her shoes. 'I'd shake your hand but I seem to be holding something just a tad heavy at the moment.'

'Oh, my goodness, I'm sorry!' She leapt to attention. 'Can you manage it?'

'I think I'll just about cope,' he said drily. 'You'll have to show me the way, though.'

'Of course—she's on the second floor,' she told him over her shoulder, heading up the stairs at a fast clip. 'Josh must be on the floor above.'

'He is. I think he's giving Milly a tour at the moment. We've finished, at last. I can't believe he thinks he needs this much.'

Cait laughed. 'We're not the only ones, then? I'm sure most of what you're struggling with is non-essential.'

'Nothing's essential,' he said drily. 'Not by the time you've lugged it up three flights of stairs.'

He lowered the box to the last square inch of space on Milly's floor, and straightened with a smile, holding out his hand. He must be fit, she thought. He isn't even breathing hard.

'It's good to meet you, Cait,' he said, and belatedly she reached out her hand and felt it totally engulfed in a warm, hard grip that robbed her of her senses. She mumbled something about small worlds, and he laughed.

'Not really. There aren't that many medical schools— you're almost bound to meet someone you know.'

'Well, I'm very glad we met you! Quite apart from you lugging that huge box upstairs for me, it's comforting to know she's not totally alone in this big, bad city.'

He shot her an understanding smile. His eyes crinkled and seemed to glow with warmth from their amber depths, and she felt herself melting again. She could still feel the imprint of his hand on hers, and something deep in her heart that had been in hibernation for ever seemed to flicker into life.

How long they stood there staring at each other she didn't know, but Milly and Josh erupted into the room and broke the spell, and a girl opposite came out and introduced herself, and suddenly Cait felt redundant.

'Time to make a move,' Owen murmured, and she nodded distractedly.

'Come on, Josh, come and see me off,' he said, and his son's face seemed to falter.

'Oh. Right. See you, Milly.'

Milly nodded, and the girl from the next room looked from her to Cait and said she'd see Milly later, and went out, leaving them alone.

'Want me to help you unpack?' Cait asked, not knowing whether to prolong the agony or get the heck out of it before she made a fool of herself.

'I can manage,' Milly said. 'It'll give me something to do until teatime.'

'Now, the phone in here should be working for me to ring in, they said, so I'll call you when I'm home, and you've got your mobile if you need me—'

'It's OK, Mum. I'll be fine.' She hugged Cait, and Cait wrapped her arms around her and thought how slight Milly felt, how small and slender and fragile and much too little to be here, doing this all on her own.

'Right, I'll be off before I get a parking ticket,' she said brightly, and kissed Milly on the cheek. 'Remember, I'm there if you need me. Love you.'

She hugged her daughter again, a brief, hard hug, and then turned and made her way sightlessly through the corridors and out into the street. The Mercedes was gone, so she backed into the space, pulled out into the street and made her way out into the hum of the London traffic.

I won't cry, she told herself firmly, and then again out loud, 'I won't cry! She's doing what she wants to do. She's happy! She's made it. There's nothing to cry about.'

But there was, of course, because her baby had grown up and flown the nest, and now Cait would be all alone.

'You'll be able to do what you've always wanted to do. You've enrolled for that course in Law, and you can read books and go to films and museums and art galleries, and do all the things you've never had time for.'

Intellectual things. Not family things. She'd be clever and better educated, but she'd be *lonely*.

She sniffed hard and scrubbed her cheeks on the back of her hand, then had to dig about in her pocket for a tissue. She wandered into the next lane and got a blast on a horn for her pains, and after that she turned on the radio and sang to it, very loudly and utterly off key, all the way out of London onto the A12.

Then finally her bravado fizzled out, and she turned off at a roadside restaurant, folded her arms on the steering wheel and laid her head down and howled.

'Idiot,' she told herself disparagingly a few minutes later. 'You must look a total fright.'

She lifted her head, blew her nose vigorously and glared at herself in the rear-view mirror. Red-rimmed, bloodshot eyes glared back at her, and she sighed unsteadily. 'Coffee,' she said, and opened the car door, to find Owen Douglas standing there, immaculately clad legs crossed at the ankle, propping up a familiar Mercedes estate.

'You OK?' he said softly, and she closed her eyes in despair. Of all the times to bump into someone you didn't know well enough to howl on.

'I'll live,' she muttered, and forced herself to meet his eyes. They were gentle with understanding, and suddenly she was glad he was there because, know him or not, he was at least in the same boat.

'You look like I feel,' he said with a rueful smile. 'How about a coffee?'

She nodded. 'I was just going in. Have you only just arrived?'

He shook his head. 'No, I was leaving. I'm in no hurry, though, and I'm sure I could force down another cup. You know what they say about misery loving company.'

Her laugh was a little strangled, and it ended on something suspiciously like a sob, but at least it was a laugh, and maybe she'd cried enough.

'Coffee sounds good,' she said, and for the first time in hours, she managed a genuine smile. 'Thanks.'

'My pleasure,' he murmured, and his voice sent little fingers of anticipation shivering up and down her spine.

Don't be a fool, he's married, she told herself fiercely, but his eyes were smiling and her heart was clearly not listening at all...

CHAPTER TWO

SHE looks gutted, Owen thought as they headed towards the restaurant. Empty and hollow and a little lost, just how he felt. He held the door for Cait and caught a drift of scent—not really perfume, just a subtle trace of something tantalising mingled with the warmth of her skin.

The waiter came up to him, looking puzzled. 'Did you leave something behind, sir?' he asked, and Owen shook his head.

'No. I've just bumped into a friend and decided to come back,' he said, and then wondered if it were rather overstating the case to call her a friend. Probably. A slight acquaintance was nearer the mark.

Very slight.

And yet he felt he knew her, because they were sharing the same very real and basic emotions at the moment and that gave them an instant connection.

He ushered her to a seat, his hand resting lightly on the smooth, supple curve of her spine, and as they sat down opposite each other she flashed him a small but potent smile that hit him right in the solar plexus.

'Thank you for rescuing me,' she said softly. 'I hate coming into places like this alone, but I couldn't go on any longer without...'

She trailed off, so he finished the sentence for her. 'Letting go?' he suggested. His grin felt crooked. 'Been there, done that.'

Cait searched his face with her luminous grey eyes, and he wondered if the few renegade tears that had escaped his rigid control had left their mark. So what if they had? he decided. He loved his son. After all they'd been through together, Josh was worthy of his tears.

'Are you OK?' she asked gently, and he gave a soft grunt of laughter.

'I'll do,' he said with a sigh, and she smiled back, tucking her long dark hair behind her ears and fiddling with her watchstrap.

'Hell, isn't it?' she said. 'I've spent years working towards this with her, and now it's come I feel—oh, I don't know what I feel.'

'Oh, I do,' he said with heartfelt sympathy. 'I know exactly how you feel.'

Her smile was a bit wonky. 'Oh, well. At least you didn't make an ass of yourself in the car park,' she told him drily, and he chuckled.

'I wouldn't bet on it.'

The waiter came up to them, pad in hand, and asked if they were ready to order.

'Coffee?' Owen suggested, and she nodded.

'Please.'

'Anything else? We could always eat if you're hungry.'

He met her eyes, those lovely soft grey eyes with the dark line defining the iris. Her skin was clear, her lips soft and mobile, and he had an insane urge to kiss them. Just now they were moving, saying something, and he had to pull himself together almost physically. 'Sorry, I didn't catch that,' he said, and she gave him an odd look.

Dear me, you're losing it, Owen, old chum, he told himself, and felt heat crawl up his neck.

'I said, I don't want to hold you up,' Cait repeated. 'Won't your wife be waiting for you?'

Jill. His embarrassment faded, replaced by the ache of an old, familiar sadness.

He shook his head. 'No. No, she won't be waiting,' he said softly. 'What about you? Will there be someone waiting for you?'

She shook her head. Something flickered briefly in her eyes that found an echo in his lonely soul. It was replaced by her slightly off-kilter smile. 'No. No one's waiting for me, except the cat, and she can cope.'

'So—how about it?'

'I tell you what, I'll bring your coffee while you decide,' the waiter said, giving up on them and handing them a menu each. Owen felt a twinge of guilt. He'd forgotten the man's existence.

'Thanks,' he murmured, and raised a brow at Cait. 'Well?'

She looked down at the menu, then up at him again. 'Um—if you've got time, I wouldn't mind something light.'

'Have whatever. I'm going for a truly wicked fry-up.'

Her eyes widened, and then she laughed, a low, musical sound that played hell with his composure. 'Comfort food?' she said wryly, and he chuckled.

'Something like that. Plus I don't have Josh nagging me. He's a health-food freak. How he'll survive in halls I can't imagine.'

'Milly will be in clover. My cooking's hit and miss at the best of times, and most of the time I'm too busy to worry. I can't remember when I last cooked anything like a roast—well, apart from last night, but it was sort of the Last Supper and the Prodigal Son all rolled into one, if you get my drift.'

He did. He'd done just the same thing, only they'd gone out to a restaurant and then on to a pub and caught a taxi home, both a little the worse for wear and a bit subdued this morning.

The waiter brought their coffee, and Owen poured them both a cup and sat back, stirring his cream in absently and thinking about Josh and how odd it was going to be at home without him.

'So, what do you do that keeps you so busy?' he asked with deliberate cheer, changing the subject, and she laughed and rolled her eyes.

'I've got a shop, for my sins—I hire and make ball gowns, and occasionally wedding dresses. It's a bit seasonal, but there's usually a steady flow of work. The balls are winter and the weddings are summer, in the main, so it pans out quite well. What about you?'

'I'm a doctor—a surgeon,' he told her. 'I cut up people instead of fabric. It's easier than your job. People heal.'

It made Cait laugh. 'True, but I can buy new fabric if I make a mess, and I can always make a mock-up,' she pointed out, and he smiled.

'I'll have to concede that one. I can't see me waking a patient up and saying, "OK, that was just a dummy run, now we'll do the real thing."'

Her smile was gorgeous. Too wide, really, but her teeth were even and sparkling, and her nose wrinkled up when she laughed. She really used the whole of her face. Every muscle of it was involved in her spontaneous expressions.

She'd be a lousy poker player, Owen thought slowly, but she'd be incredible to make love to. Every touch, every stroke would find an echo in that wonderfully mobile face and those incredible eyes.

He shifted slightly in his seat, aware of the stirrings of a need he hadn't felt in years. She worried her bottom lip with her teeth, and his breath jammed in his lungs. He dragged his eyes from her face and down to the menu, scanning it blindly for a moment until his eyes focused. Then he chose the most wicked thing he could find and stuck the menu back in the holder.

'I'm ready when you are,' he told her, his voice sounding strangled, and the double meaning hit him like a tram. Oh, hell. He hoped she wasn't looking at him, because for a brief, terrifying second he was sure his thoughts were clearly written on his face—and they were seriously, seriously X-rated!

Cait was starving.

Owen had chosen what he was having and had put his menu down, but she was torn between the toast and pâté she'd spotted at first and the wonderful illustration of golden crispy chicken and chips with a side salad. It was horribly expensive by comparison, but what the heck. She could afford to splash out every once in a while, and it was a rather unique occasion, if not exactly special in the accepted sense!

'I can't decide,' she murmured, but her eyes strayed back to the chicken and chips. 'I was going to have the pâté, but this looks so tempting…'

'Go for it,' he advised, taking the menu out of her hand. 'Stop worrying. Instinct is a wonderful thing.'

'So it is. OK, I'll go for it.'

She looked up into his face, but it was expressionless, apart from a polite smile that told her nothing. He hailed the waiter, ordered their meal and topped up her coffee.

She stirred the cream into it, chasing a bubble round

the top, and then looked up at him again, surprising an unguarded look that made her breath catch in her throat.

No. She was imagining it. Of course he hadn't looked at her like that.

'So, where do you live?' she asked to fill the silence, and then wondered if that was too intrusive a question to ask on such brief acquaintance. Apparently not, because Owen volunteered the information without a flicker.

'Just south of Audley—about ten miles out, a little bit west of Wenham Market.'

'That's near me,' she said, and wondered if she sounded hopelessly over-eager. That would be embarrassing. Just because he'd said there was no one waiting that didn't mean there was no one in his life. Maybe she was away, perhaps on business. Oh, blast.

'Near you?' he said. 'The shop or your house?'

'Both. That's where the shop is, in the square, between the antique shop and the butcher, and we live in the flat above it.'

'It's a nice little town—or is it a village?'

Cait laughed softly. 'I don't know. I'm not sure they can decide. We've got a village hall, but it's quite big for a village and it's got lots of shops. I'd say it was more of a town, in a way.'

'It's got lots of character. I envy you in a way. It's a bit isolated where we are. It's all part of its essential charm, but it's also one of the greatest drawbacks.'

'Is it an old house?' she asked, slightly appalled at her curiosity, but he didn't seem to mind.

'Yes and no,' he said confusingly, and then elaborated with a smile. 'It's a converted barn—so the barn itself is old, but it's only been a house for a short while. Six years or so, I think. I bought it three years ago, after my wife died.'

Cait felt shock run over her like iced water. Not away on business, then, she thought numbly, and shook her head in denial. 'Oh, Owen, I'm so sorry,' she murmured.

'Why should you be sorry?' he said softly. 'It's just one of those things. It was quick, at least. She didn't suffer. She had a burst blood vessel in the brain—she must have died almost instantly.'

'Oh, Owen,' she said again. 'How awful for you. Was she at home?'

'No. She was in the car. She'd pulled over but the engine was still running. A witness said she pulled up, slumped over and that was it. They discovered the haemorrhage at post-mortem.'

How hideous for them. How horribly sudden and violent and unexpected. She felt tears prickle at the back of her eyes and blinked them away. 'It must have been dreadful,' she said, choked. 'How did Josh take it?'

Owen laughed, a short, humourless huff of sound. 'Not well. He was fourteen at the time. He was furious with her.'

'And the others—are there any others?'

He shook his head. 'No. No others. Just me and Josh.'

'Chicken and chips?'

They both looked up, slightly startled, to see the waiter hovering over them with two plates.

'Um—yes, thank you,' Cait said, moving her cup out of the way and letting his revelation sink in. The waiter left them, and without thinking she reached out her hand and covered his. 'Owen—thanks for telling me about it.'

His grin was crooked and a little off-key. 'That's OK. I don't usually talk about it. I'm sorry to unravel on you like that. I shouldn't have brought it up.'

'Yes, you should. She was a part of your life for years. You can't just not talk about her as if she didn't exist.'

He met her steady gaze, gratitude at her understanding showing in his amber eyes, and then he smiled a little sadly. 'Thank you for that. You're right, but most people don't see it that way. It makes them uncomfortable.'

'That's silly.'

'Maybe. Eat your chicken and chips.'

She looked at his plate, heaped with what looked for all the world like a truly wicked Sunday breakfast, and had a sudden urge to dunk her chip in his egg yolk.

'Go on, then, if you must.'

'What?' She looked up, startled, to find him laughing softly at her.

'Dunk your chips in my egg.'

The smile wouldn't be held in. 'That's so rude of me. How did you know?'

'Something to do with the longing look you gave it?'

Oh, lord. She'd better not direct any longing looks at *him*, then. He was altogether too good at picking them up!

She reached over, the chip in her fingers, and pierced the golden yolk. 'Oh, yum,' she mumbled round the mouthful, and he laughed again.

'One more, and that's your lot,' he said firmly, and she indulged herself one last time before turning her attention to the fragrant, steaming plateful of chicken in front of her.

Within a few minutes she'd demolished it, and sat back with a huge sigh of contentment. 'Oh, wow,' she said with a grin. 'Excellent.'

He speared the last mushroom and chewed it thoughtfully, then smiled back. 'How about a pud?'

'That's too wicked!' She laughed. 'Anyway, I'll burst.'

'How horribly messy. We'd better avoid that at all costs. Another coffee?'

She shook her head, reality coming back to her. She had work to do before she opened the shop in the morning, and it was already after seven. Besides, the cat would be hungry and would take the hump and go off in a sulk if she didn't get back soon.

'I ought to go,' she told him, and he nodded.

'OK.' He looked up and caught the waiter's eye, and a bill appeared a moment later.

'Could you please split it?' she asked him, but Owen shook his head.

'No. Leave it. Here.' He counted out a pile of notes, told the man to keep the change and ushered her out.

'You shouldn't have done that,' she protested, but he just smiled.

'Yes, I should. I talked you into it—and, anyway, it was a pleasure having your company.' He walked her to her car, and as she reached it he looked down into her eyes and searched them in silence for a moment.

'Thank you for rescuing me from the doldrums,' she said, a touch breathlessly, and he smiled, just a slight shift of his lips in the harsh glare of the outside lights. His eyes were in shadow, but they seemed to burn with an inner fire that she didn't dare interpret.

'My pleasure,' he murmured, and before she could move or speak or even blink, he bent his head and brushed her lips with his. 'Goodnight, Cait. Take care.'

He slipped a card into her hand. 'Here. This is my number. Ring me if you need anything.'

Then he was gone, his long legs striding round his car. He slid behind the wheel and waited for her to get into her car, then once she was settled and pulled forward a fraction, he raised a hand in farewell and followed her out of the car park.

His lights trailed her all the way home, then as she pulled up they flashed a couple of times and he drove away.

How chivalrous, she thought with a tiny smile, and then looked up at the dark window in her flat over the shop. Oh, lord. No Milly to nag and bully and hug. None of her various friends to trip over, no festering coffee-mugs on Milly's bedroom window-sill, no frenzied searching for a bag, a phone, a piece of paper.

Just silence.

Cait braced herself, and got out of the car. It was time to start the rest of her life.

She slid her hand into her pocket to pull out her house keys, and the sharp corner of Owen's card scratched the palm of her hand. She pulled it out and looked at it in the dim light of the streetlamps, and a smile curved her lips.

Maybe—just maybe—her new life had already started.

CHAPTER THREE

CAIT would have gone crazy in the next few days without the cat to keep her company. They were both a little lost without Milly, and to comfort herself poor old Bagpuss took up residence in Cait's immediate vicinity.

Wherever she was, the cat was too. She slept with her, she followed her round all day, and she cried piteously if Cait shut her out.

It was getting on her nerves, but since she could understand it, it was hard to get cross with her.

Well, most of the time. On the second Sunday Milly was gone, she put down a wedding dress for ten seconds and came back to find the cat making a nest inside the piles of tulle.

'Out!' she ordered firmly, not daring to pick the cat up for fear of plucking the fine netting, and Bagpuss stalked off with her tail in the air. It didn't last long, though. Within moments she was back again, scratching at the door until Cait relented and let her back in.

She jumped up and settled down on the sewing table next to the pins and bobbins, tucking her paws under her and purring gloatingly because she'd got her own way again. Every now and again she reached out an idle paw and batted at the threads trailing from the needles in the pin cushion, making Cait nervous. She moved the pin cushion out of reach.

'I don't need a vet bill,' she said, but the cat just washed herself and settled down for a snooze. 'Tired?' Cait asked unfeelingly. 'That's because you were miaowing all night and keeping me awake. I told you, she's gone. She won't be back for ages. Maybe even Christmas.'

Christmas? Good grief. It seemed such a long time away, but it wasn't really. She was just finishing off this last of a run of wedding dresses, and then she'd have to overhaul her winter ball gowns, all the reds and blacks and deep greens that were so popular for the Christmas balls.

Some would need revamping, others would go in the pre-season sale, and she would have to do a lot of re-stocking, so she wouldn't have time to miss Milly.

Not really. Only every time she got out two plates for supper, or cooked two jacket potatoes instead of one, or weighed out the wrong amount of spaghetti. Only whenever she went into the bathroom and it was tidy, with no soggy towels dropped on the floor or nightdress abandoned over the edge of the bath or the scales missing.

Only whenever she heard something funny and wanted to share it with her daughter, and then remembered she wasn't there.

She was getting on fine, by all accounts—or at least she seemed to be. She'd rung a couple of times, between one party and another, and she seemed to be having a great time.

Unlike Cait, who was submerged under a pile of tulle that had to be ready by tomorrow.

And then, of course, there was the evening class she'd enrolled herself on.

She sighed. Maybe she was trying to take too much

on, but she couldn't afford to get someone else to run the shop and she didn't dare farm out the sewing. She'd tried that before, with disastrous consequences.

So she'd struggle, and she'd probably have to stay up half the night every now and again, but she'd get there.

She had an essay to finish for tomorrow night, come to that, but her bride was coming for a fitting at nine in the morning, and she had to get the dress to the right stage by then. Still, it was straightforward enough, a variation on a pattern she'd made several times before.

She stayed up until eleven working on it, then started on the essay. Not a good move. Her brain felt like treacle, and the words seemed doubly impenetrable through the fog of exhaustion.

She fell asleep with her head in the book at one, went to bed and tried to carry on, and finally at three she admitted defeat, turned out the light and disappeared into blissful oblivion until eight thirty-eight.

Twenty-two minutes till her fitting.

Great!

She shot out of bed, had the fastest shower in the history of mankind and gave the cat a double portion of food by accident as she rushed out of the flat and downstairs to the shop, the dress carefully held aloft so she didn't trip over it and shred the bottom.

Her bride was late. Almost half an hour late—time for a cup of tea and some toast while she finished off her essay, had she but known, but she didn't, so she spent the whole time waiting for the young woman to arrive.

Still, she got the shop tidied after Saturday's hectic rummaging and started her winter stock check, so the time wasn't exactly wasted, although it was a bit irritating because it was Monday and the shop was shut on Mondays except for fittings and for regular clients who couldn't come on any other day. She could have been having a lie-in, she thought resentfully, or finishing the darned essay.

Her bride arrived, and the dress, by a miracle, was wonderful on her, elegant and flattering to a figure that was less than perfect, and she was ecstatic. Good, Cait thought, I'll get paid, and then just as she was seeing her off and locking the shop again, a car pulled up outside.

She just caught a glimpse of it out of the corner of her eye, and her heart sank. Not another customer. Not today, when she had the essay to do!

She turned back to the door and her heart zoomed back up out of her boots and started hammering away at the base of her throat.

Owen—here, of all places, out of the blue and unheralded, when she'd just dragged a comb through her wet hair and pulled on the first clean clothes on hand. Why was he always destined to see her at her worst?

She glanced down at her jeans and sweater and shrugged. Perhaps not her very worst. At least the sweater didn't have holes in it and the jeans were the ones that fitted her bottom nicely. Pity about the make-up, but two out of three wasn't bad and it *was* lovely to see him again.

Very lovely. Wonderful, in fact, she realised, as her heart skittered about and did strange things to her insides.

Trying not to grin too inanely, she opened the door again and leant against the doorframe, her arms folded across her chest, one leg resting slightly bent against the other. 'Hi, there,' she said, feeling the smile widen despite her best efforts. 'Don't tell me, you want a ball gown.'

He grinned back. 'Shucks, you guessed. Still, it can be our little secret. I thought something off the shoulder…?'

She felt one eyebrow climb, and her lips twitched. 'Come in, I'll see what I can do for you.'

'Too kind.'

He walked past her into the shop, passing within millimetres of her, and all her senses screamed to full alert. Suddenly the shop seemed absurdly small and crowded.

Cait turned the lock on the door and eyed him blatantly, disguising her sudden confusion with a jokey appraisal of his body. 'Mmm. Those shoulders could be a problem,' she teased, and he smiled.

'Ah, well. Never mind the gown, I'll settle for a coffee.'

A coffee. She had tea, she had hot chocolate. Coffee she was out of—and the kitchen looked as if a bomb had gone off in it. 'Um—' she flannelled, but he cut her off.

'I've got the day off. I just called on spec because I thought you'd be in, but—as you're shut—maybe we could go out—if you'd like to, that is, or you've got time?'

'Out?' she said blankly, and could have kicked herself for sounding so vacant.

'Out—you know, maybe to the seaside or a craft centre or something? I don't know. Whatever you fancy.'

He sounded a little lost, and she tipped her head on one side and studied him thoughtfully. 'You miss him, don't you?'

Owen's mouth kicked up at the side and he gave a short huff of laughter. 'Rumbled,' he said wryly, and searched her face. 'How about you?'

Cait shrugged. 'It seems very odd. She's rung me a couple of times, when she's been able to fit it in—they seem to do nothing but go from one party to another. I can't get her on her room phone at all.'

'Ditto. Josh says the medics really know how to party. I don't think he's been to bed for more than a hour at a time for the last week and a half.' He shoved his hands into his pockets and rocked back on his heels. 'So—fancy playing hookey?'

Her mouth tipped in a slow smile. 'Do I ever,' she said with feeling. 'I have an essay to finish for tonight for my Law evening class, I have to put that wedding dress together now she's had a fitting, and the place is a tip. Oh, yes, I fancy playing hookey—in capitals!'

He laughed. 'Let's go, then.'

'I need to change,' she said, eyeing his suit, but he shook his head.

'No. You're fine. I wish I was wearing something less formal. I hate suits.'

'So why did you put it on?' she asked, puzzled.

'Because my day off was unscheduled. They had to close my theatre because of staff shortages, so my list was cancelled at the last minute. I suppose we could go via my house and I could change. How long can you spare?'

Cait thought of everything she had to do, and then thought of the rest of her life spent doing just that, and smiled defiantly. 'As long as you like.'

He nodded, a smile hovering in his eyes. 'OK. We'll go via mine and I'll change. You can meet the dogs then—are you all right with dogs?'

'I love dogs,' she told him. 'I just can't have one in the flat. The garden's tiny and it's not really fair when I'm at work all day, even if it is just downstairs.'

Owen pulled a thoughtful face and nodded again, slowly. 'I agree. I didn't know what to do about mine when Jill died, but I think they'd probably rather stay with me and put up with my long hours at work than be rehomed, and anyway, I'd miss them. Still, I have a home help who comes in every day for a couple of hours, so it's not too bad.'

Every day, Cait thought enviously. She'd give her eye teeth for someone to come and run a vacuum over the flat once a month, never mind every day. She kept the shop immaculate, but the flat always seemed to run away with her. Ah, well.

'What do I need?' she asked, and he shrugged.

'Coat? Shoes for walking if you fancy walking, or not if you don't. Nothing much.'

She nodded. 'Give me five seconds and I'll be back,' she said, and then threw over her shoulder as she headed for the door marked PRIVATE, 'You could pick out your ball gown while you're waiting!'

She ran up to the flat, apologised to Bagpuss for deserting her and dithered for a moment over her make-up. No, too obvious, she decided, and grabbed a coat and her trainers and bag and ran back down.

'I thought this one,' he said, holding up a few strips of gold held together with imagination. It was an outrageous gown and just the thought of Owen in it made her lips twitch.

She shook her head. 'No. You need a bigger bust to carry it off,' she told him, deadpan.

He hung it up again, pulling a regretful face, and she laughed.

'Ah, poor baby,' she teased, and his mouth quirked.

'You're a hard woman—I'm sure my bust is big enough for that dress.'

'You'd have to wax your chest, though,' she pointed out wickedly, and he winced.

'Perhaps not, then. I'll stick to the DJ.'

'Might be safer.'

Cait locked the shop behind them, and he settled her into the luxury of the passenger seat before going round and sliding behind the wheel. The car purred to life and slid out seamlessly into the traffic, and she settled back against the seat and allowed herself to be pampered.

Soft music flowed around them, and as he drove they chatted about this and that. He was so easy to talk to, she thought, with his teasing sense of humour and his ready wit, but there was so much more to him, such depth and breadth and a wonderful human warmth that drew her like a moth to a flame.

Don't start having fantasies about him, she warned herself, but it was pointless. Every moment in his company she felt herself drawn closer to him, and by the time they arrived at his house she knew she was in deep trouble.

For the first time in her life, she realised, she was in serious danger of falling in love. Not lust, not a teenage crush or the hopeful dreams of a lonely young mother, but love.

And only a fool would allow herself to fall in love with a man who was so clearly out of reach.

CHAPTER FOUR

IT WAS a wonderful house. Snuggled into the side of a hill off a winding country lane, the old half-timbered barn looked out over the gently rolling farmland to the woods on the far side.

Autumn colour was just beginning to touch the leaves, and Cait guessed that in a few weeks the blaze of colour would be spectacular. In between, the land was freshly ploughed, the turned earth like rich, dark chocolate, and in the distance she could see a tractor moving slowly across a field, seagulls swooping and fluttering in its wake like the tail of a kite.

She breathed deeply of the fresh country air and thought of Josh and Milly stuck in the middle of London, surrounded by all those fumes, and she wanted to cry for them.

Owen opened the door and held out an arm to her, beckoning her inside with a smile. 'Come on in—dogs, get down!' he said, and the dogs subsided, wagging round them both and sniffing her with interest. 'They're just checking you out, they won't hurt you,' he told her, not that she needed reassuring. She guessed she was more in danger of being licked to death. 'This one's Daisy, the other one's Jess. Say hello nicely, girls.'

Cait looked at them, identical chocolate Labradors, and wondered how on earth he could tell the difference.

'Different collars,' he explained, reading her mind, and she laughed and patted them, introducing herself and trying to learn the difference, and then she straightened up and saw the interior of the barn, and fell in love all over again.

'Oh, wow,' she said softly, her breath almost taken away. They were in a lobby near one end, and through the open doorway she could see a wonderfully cosy sitting room at the end nearest her, and then beyond an open studwork partition the dining room soaring to the roof, with huge windows on both sides stretching up to the eaves.

A massive stove squatted between the two rooms, a gleaming stainless steel stovepipe emerging from the top of it and stretching up towards the roof. At the far end of the dining room two steps rose to the kitchen, with more open studwork to divide it from the central area.

'Come on in,' he said.

She followed Owen through the cosy and inviting sitting room into the central dining room, and tilting her head back she looked up into the great beamed vault of the roof. The ends were divided off with closed studwork, the beams still visible, so that over the kitchen and sitting room were two rooms, presumably bedrooms, and between them a walkway was suspended from the tie beams by steel rods, accessed by a sweeping spiral staircase in gleaming steel.

It was a fascinating mix of ancient and modern—sort of high tech meets country, Cait thought, and then she moved her head and caught a glimpse of the view through the wall of glass, and she was spellbound.

'Oh, it's gorgeous!' she said with feeling.

'You like it?' he asked, sounding curiously vulnerable. She turned to him in amazement.

'Like it? It's wonderful! Of course I like it!'

'Not everybody does. Bit rustic. Jill wouldn't have liked it—she used to say she couldn't understand why anyone would want to live in a shed.'

Hence the vulnerability. Oh, yipes.

'Maybe it wasn't her kind of thing,' she said carefully, anxious not to criticise the dead woman. 'It might be a bit…informal for some tastes.'

Owen nodded. 'She liked order and everything in its place. We had a big Victorian house in the town before—formal and elegant and no surprises—and for all she loved them to bits, the dogs weren't allowed out of the kitchen and breakfast areas.'

'And now I suppose they sleep on your bed,' she teased.

He laughed softly. 'No. Just the settees. It's a bit hard to stop them when there isn't a door to close, but I don't care. It's not a showpiece, it's a home.'

'I think it's gorgeous,' she said, wondering how to ask him to show her round and unable to say the words. She didn't know him well enough, and it was such an intrusion.

'You want a guided tour?'

She pulled a wry face. 'I'm sorry. Is it so obvious?'

Owen laughed. 'Don't worry. I know what it's like. I love looking at other people's houses. It's so revealing.'

Thank goodness I didn't let him up into the flat this morning, then, she thought with a bubble of hysterical laughter threatening. Revealing wasn't in it. He would have run a mile!

He took her through the ground floor first, back past the front door in the lobby and through to a pair of bedrooms each with doors out to the garden and their own shower room just next to them. 'Josh has this bit of the house,' he explained, but it was self-evident in the posters and clutter and general abundance of teenage gear, even without all the things he'd taken away.

'What a good idea,' she said, regretting the smallness of her flat. 'It must be more peaceful. Milly's music drives me potty.'

He laughed. 'Ditto. The house isn't very good at being soundproof with all the open studwork. This way I didn't have to listen to *his* dreadful choice in music.'

They retraced their footsteps back through the sitting room and dining room and into the kitchen. While Cait looked round enviously at all the cupboards and conjured with the very thought of having enough room for a central work island, he put the kettle on the Aga and gave her a quick glance at the pantry and utility room, then he led her up the staircase to the bedrooms.

'This is the spare room,' he said, taking her along the walkway to the one over the sitting room.

'Oh, it's huge!' Cait said, looking round at the four-poster bed nestled under the roof, with the window opposite so you could lie in bed in the morning and look at the woods and the fields and wallow in the beauty of it all.

'Why don't you sleep in here?' she asked, sticking her head round the door of the *en suite* bathroom. 'It's gorgeous.'

'I know. It's a lovely room and it's got a fabulous view, but I prefer the other one. It's over the Aga and it's warmer, and it's got a funny door. It just appeals to me.'

She followed him back down the walkway to the other room, and he pointed out the door that was cut along the top to fit the contours of the beam. She had to duck to clear the beam, and climb three little steps, and then they were in his bedroom.

The bed was huge, and yet it seemed scarcely big enough for the vast expanse of space. A row of doors in aged oak led to the little shower room, the loo and the walk-in wardrobe down one side, and on the other was a window criss-crossed with beams, looking out over the valley again.

Owen glanced round and rubbed his chin ruefully. 'I'm sorry, it's not exactly tidy. Mrs Poole doesn't arrive until eleven and I left in a bit of a hurry this morning, so I didn't make the bed.'

'Don't apologise—I didn't make mine, either,' she said with a laugh, but her eye was drawn to the tousled quilt and the dented pillow, and she felt a shiver of hot and cold run over her. Suddenly the enormous room seemed tiny and Owen seemed very, very close—scarily close, and extremely male.

I'm going to make a fool of myself, Cait thought, but then a noise caught her attention, a high-pitched whistle, and he turned towards the door.

'The kettle's boiling,' he said. 'Mind your head on the way out.'

'Why don't I go and take it off while you change?' she suggested, and he turned on the steps and bumped into her, reaching up to steady her.

Their eyes locked, and Cait couldn't breathe. Oh, lord, now what? she thought, but he seemed to pull himself together visibly. 'Good idea,' he said, and stepped back, knocking his head on a beam behind him.

He ducked and swore softly, and Cait made her escape down the stairs to the kitchen, stifling a chuckle.

The dogs were bracketing the Aga, and she stepped over them to remove the kettle. 'I hope you really are friendly,' she said, and they thumped their tails and grinned at her. 'I take it that's a yes.'

'Coffee's in the cupboard next to the Aga,' Owen called down. 'Instant or real—take your pick. There are teabags, too. The fridge is in the corner.'

'Thanks,' she called back, suddenly aware of how close he was and what he was doing. Excitement tingled along her veins, and she tried not to think about him changing his clothes so very close to her. She could hear the odd clonk that was probably shoes coming off or going on, and drawers and doors opening and shutting, and the slight creak of the bed as he sat on it.

There had been a towel draped over the end of the bed, but she hadn't noticed any pyjamas lying around. Did that mean he slept naked? Heat shimmered over her skin, and she slapped her wrist.

'Cait, behave,' she told herself fiercely. 'It's none of your business.'

But she wanted it to be. For the first time in her adult life, she really, really wanted to develop a relationship with a man—this man, this funny, sensitive, generous man with eyes like molten toffee and lips she was aching to kiss...

Owen sat on the edge of the bed and sighed. He was going to make an idiot of himself over her, just because she was warm and gentle and funny and seemed totally unaware of how lovely she was.

He'd nearly kissed her when he'd turned on the steps and bumped into her, and her mouth had been just there in front of his, soft and slightly parted with surprise, and the longing had hit him like a thunderbolt.

Then he'd leapt out of the way and crowned himself

on that beam, and she'd run down to the kitchen, no doubt splitting her sides laughing at him.

He rubbed the back of his head ruefully and sighed again. Damn. He had a bruise. Oh, well, it would serve him right—remind him not to make an idiot of himself. Or at least a worse idiot than he already had. He tugged on his jeans and a thick rugby shirt, pulled a sweater out of the drawer and put on his comfortable old shoes, then ran down to the kitchen.

'What did you make?' he asked, but she just smiled that lovely wide smile and shook her head, and heat slammed through him.

'Nothing. I didn't know what you'd want. I'll make it now, if you like.'

Suddenly the kitchen seemed terribly small and intimate, and with nobody else around to dilute the atmosphere he could hardly breathe. Plus any minute now Mrs Poole would be here, and he couldn't cope with her insatiable curiosity. 'Let's go out,' he suggested rapidly. 'We'll get coffee somewhere—unless you'd rather not?'

She shook her head again. 'I don't mind. Whatever.'

'We'll go out,' he said, more firmly, and headed for the door.

Was it something she'd said? Owen seemed preoccupied and uncomfortable, and Cait wondered if it was because she'd said she liked the barn and reminded him about his wife.

Had he taken her remarks as a criticism? Surely not—she'd only said she liked the house, but maybe he felt guilty because he liked it, too, and if Jill wouldn't have done—oh, it was hopeless. She couldn't work it out, she didn't know enough about him, so she sat quietly beside him as he drove across to the coast, and they walked along the front at Aldeburgh in the keen October wind, and when their fingers and noses were frozen they took refuge in a hotel bar for coffee.

He seemed more relaxed now, and so she found herself able to relax and enjoy his company. He was very easy to talk to, and after a while she found herself talking about Milly.

'I was so worried about how she'd cope, but she seems to be having loads of fun. Partying till dawn, by all accounts. I don't know, I never had so much fun when I was her age—well, of course I didn't, because I had her running around underfoot all day and night.'

He studied her thoughtfully over his coffee cup. 'You must have been very young when you had her,' he said in a gentle voice totally devoid of criticism. 'It must have been hard.'

'It was. I was seventeen—just. My parents were in the throes of splitting up, my boyfriend's parents had split up—we were in the same boat, really, and I suppose we just turned to each other for comfort. Anyway, when I found I was pregnant my parents went off at the deep end and threw me out, and he was sent away to sixth-form college, and that was the end of that. He wrote for a while, but he never sees her and he's living abroad so I don't get any financial help from him. I never have had—well, that's not quite true. He sent her a cheque for a hundred pounds for her eighteenth birthday and she gave it to me because she said she didn't want it and my car needed servicing.'

Oh, dear. She hadn't meant to tell him that, to let him know how close she came to the wire in a bad month, or what a knife-edge they lived on. She had no sickness insurance, so if she had to have time off—well, she couldn't, and she'd always managed to struggle downstairs to the shop no matter how bad she'd felt, and luckily she'd been reasonably well.

The threat was there, though, and it worried her, but it wasn't Owen's business, and he didn't need to know.

'I thought we were young, at twenty-one,' he told her, and she did a quick calculation that made him thirty-nine, just four years older than her. 'How on earth did you manage? At least we had help from our parents, and we had each other. It must have been a nightmare on your own.'

Cait nodded agreement. 'I stayed with a friend until the baby was born, then the council gave me a flat, and I started doing alterations and making clothes for people. I picked up an old sewing machine and someone gave me an overlocker that didn't work, and I got it mended for a few pounds and used it for years.'

'So what gave you the idea of the shop?' he asked curiously, and she smiled.

'Money. A friend asked me to make her a ball gown, and said she'd gone to a hire shop and the cost was outrageous. I made the dress for less than the cost of the hire, and she said it was one of the nicest at the ball. Some of her friends came to me, and then they didn't want them again and started to swap, and I thought, if I had a hire shop, I could appeal to a wider market.'

'So you opened the shop.'

'Yes—and I've been there ever since. It's been wonderful, because living overhead I could work in the holidays without compromising Milly's safety, and it was within walking distance of her school and friends without being in a town centre, and it's got parking outside for customers—it's perfect.'

'Don't you get cabin fever?' he asked with a little smile, and she laughed.

'Every day. Still, I do what I have to do, and it's a lovely little place. I've got friends who drop in for coffee, and one of them will mind the shop for me if we go on holiday or go out for the day. It's OK.'

'I think you're amazing,' he said softly. 'To do what you've done for Milly, to hold the two of you together from the age of seventeen, to give her the chances you've given her with so little help—that takes a special kind of woman. I take my hat off to you. You're one gutsy lady, Cait Cooper, and you have my unqualified admiration.'

Soft colour flooded her cheeks, and she looked down, embarrassed and yet deeply touched by his praise. 'Thank you,' she said, her voice slightly choked, and he set his cup down and stood up.

'Come on, let's go back to the car and find somewhere for lunch—unless you want to go back?'

No, of course she didn't want to go back. She never wanted to go back.

'I have an essay waiting for me, remember, but I dare say it'll keep that long.'

His smile was warm and coaxing. 'I'm sure it will. Come on. You've spent eighteen years towing the line. It's time to cut yourself a little slack.'

'But the evening class was supposed to be for me!'

'It's work!' he said disgustedly. 'You need to learn how to play.'

'That's easy to say, but I don't have a playmate,' she said without thinking.

'Oh, yes, you do,' he said, and he sounded almost excited. 'I've been working too hard as well. Why don't we have our own Freshers' week? The kids are having all this fun—how about us? We could do all the things they're doing—the pub crawl, the balls, the floating restaurant, the fancy-dress party—all of it. What do you say?'

She laughed. 'You're crazy,' she told him, half-tempted. 'You're absolutely nuts.'

'No, I'm not. I had to grow up too fast, too soon, just like you. Now Jill's gone and Josh is away, and there's nothing left. It's time to start again, Cait—for both of us. Let's go for it.'

She looked up into his amazing liquid toffee eyes and was lost.

'OK,' she said slowly, and wondered just how long it would be before he broke her heart.

CHAPTER FIVE

'SO, WHAT are we doing tonight?'

Cait laughed and shook her head at Owen. 'No. I have to go to my evening class.'

'I thought we'd discussed this?' he said with a grin, but she shook her head again.

'No, you told me it was work, and it *is* work, but it's work for me and not just for the coffers, and that's different. Anyway, I'm enjoying it,' she lied. 'Another night.'

'Tomorrow?'

'I've got to finish that wedding dress. It'll take me all week.'

'Friday, then,' he said promptly. 'We'll start on Friday—and no more excuses.'

She couldn't help her answering smile. 'No excuses,' she agreed.

There was a pause, and then his hands came up and cupped her shoulders, and he lowered his mouth to hers—just briefly, the merest brush of his lips, but it sent fire skittering through her body. He lifted his head, and his eyes were molten gold.

'I'll see you on Friday,' he said huskily, and turned away, leaving her propping herself up against the shop door because her legs had simply stopped working and if she moved she'd fall over.

He drove away with a lift of his hand, and she watched him go before turning and letting herself inside. She went up to the flat on her rubbery legs and looked around, and thought what a dismal and tired little place it was after his barn.

She'd done her best with it, making curtains and loose covers to brighten it up, but when you were starting from something pretty ordinary it was hard to make it special. Perhaps it was time to decorate it—go for a new look, perhaps?

Or perhaps it was time to write her essay before her evening class started in three hours!

Owen phoned on Friday at five to ask what time he should pick her up, and told her to wear something nice.

'What are we doing?' she asked.

'Milly and Josh are going to a toga party,' he told her. 'I thought we could do a modern version.'

'Of a *toga party*!' she all but shrieked.

His chuckle came down the line. 'Don't worry, I'm not going to strut around doing Charlton Heston impressions. I thought we could go to that floating Italian restaurant for dinner.'

'What's that got to do with togas?' she asked warily.

'Nothing. Modern-day Romans.'

She felt her shoulders drop with relief. 'So, how smart?' she asked, mentally scanning her rather slight wardrobe.

'How smart do you want to be? It can be quite dressy there.'

She'd drawn a blank on her own wardrobe, but she did have a rather lovely little black dress in stock downstairs—

'Dressy will do fine,' she said, suddenly decided. 'Pick me up whenever. Do you have a reservation?'

'No—I'll make one and call you back.'

By the time he rang, she'd dashed down to the shop, rummaged through the rails and found the dress. She'd just slipped it over her head when the phone rang, and she picked it up and said 'Hello?' a little breathlessly.

'Been running?' Owen teased, and she laughed and put her hand over her chest to steady her pounding heart that owed much more to the sound of his voice than the exercise.

'I was trying on a dress,' she told him, turning this way and that and looking at it in the mirror. Good grief. She really ought to put on proper clothes more often, they made her feel wonderful!

'How does seven sound?' he asked, and she had to bite her tongue so she didn't tell him it was too soon. She had to shower and wash her hair, and inevitably it would refuse to behave and so she'd have to put it up, and she had no idea where her make-up was or if Milly had 'borrowed' it and taken it to London—

'Seven's fine,' she lied, and then ran round like a headless chicken, panicking.

Still, she was ready at a quarter to seven and had to force herself to sit still and not haunt the window looking out for him. Even so, she saw the sweep of Owen's headlights as he came into the little square, and she grabbed her coat and bag and ran down the stairs, locking the shop door behind her just as he stepped out of the car.

She stopped in her tracks. He was wearing a dinner jacket and black bow-tie on crisp white, and she could see the gleam of his shoes from where she was standing. He looked gorgeous, and her heart began to hammer.

'Hi, there,' she said with a dredged-up smile, and he smiled back a little distractedly.

His eyes scanned her and then came back and locked with hers. 'You look beautiful,' he said softly, and she felt the colour rise in her cheeks and take the place of the blusher she hadn't been able to find.

No matter. If he kept paying her compliments like that, she'd never need it again!

Cait was stunning. All week long she'd been on his mind, her courage and her determination astounding him. Most girls in her situation would have taken the easy way out, but she'd hung on and had had her baby and raised a young woman to be proud of, at the cost of her own youth.

Well, he couldn't give her back her youth, but he could give it his best shot, and he had spent the week dreaming up a whole plethora of things he could do with her. He'd jotted down a list of things Josh had told him they'd done, and he'd racked his brains to find adult equivalents.

He'd come up with something for most of them, but he'd drawn a blank on a respectable and acceptable version of licking vodka jelly off each other! He thought maybe he'd save that one for later on.

Much later on!

In the meantime, he was faced with the most beautiful woman he'd seen in a long, long time, and he didn't know if it was because she was classically beautiful, which she wasn't, or if it was because of the glow in her skin and the light in her eyes and the way her mouth trembled in that shy smile when he complimented her.

There was a staggering innocence about her, a virginal quality that brought out the chivalrous hero in him and subdued the caveman who wanted nothing more than to drag her off to his cave and make babies with her. Even so, standing here looking at her in that incredibly sexy little dress, he could hear the caveman roaring with frustration.

Down, boy, he cautioned. Allowing himself the privilege of dropping a light kiss on her cheek, he ushered her into the car and drove her to the docks. He parked near the restaurant at the back of a friend's gallery, and they strolled arm in arm along the water's edge to the converted barge that housed their destination.

Their table was by a window, and they could see the lights of the converted maltings opposite reflected in the ruffled water. There was soft music playing in the background, and everything they said seemed wittier than usual.

Finally, though, their meal was over and they'd drained the coffee-pot, and she looked round the nearly empty restaurant and smiled sadly. 'I suppose we ought to go,' she said, and she sounded regretful.

Owen hailed the waiter, unwilling to let the evening end, and after paying the bill he drew her to her feet. 'Come on,' he said, 'the night's still young.'

'It's nearly eleven!' she protested.

'Perfect. We're going clubbing.'

'Clubbing!' she squeaked, making the other diners look up in surprise. She blushed and he hid a smile and put his arm round her shoulders and led her down to the lower deck and out onto the dockside.

'Clubbing,' he repeated. 'It's over-thirties night, and we both qualify. Come on, you were complaining you hadn't lived.'

'I was?' she said with a laugh. 'I haven't been clubbing for about fifteen years!'

'Well, it's high time you did.' Owen turned her collar up against the cold, tucked her under his arm and they strolled down the dock to the centre of the local night-spots. The music was loud, the beat heavy and insistent, and he drew her into his arms on the dance floor and felt the caveman roar to life.

Cait moved like a dancer, her body fluid and supple, and her head found a natural resting place in the hollow of his shoulder. He forced the caveman back under control, and cradled her against his chest. She was too sweet and innocent to deal with the raging need that was surfacing in him, and he kept it firmly at bay, denying his urge to rock her hard against his aching body.

The tempo changed, to his relief, and became faster, and he released her and instead had to endure the torture of watching her body move to the music. Then it slowed again, and she went back into his arms, and he gave in and held her close, and for an instant he felt her stiffen with shock as she became aware of his arousal.

Then she moved closer, her body relaxing against him, and he rested his head against hers and let out his breath in a long, ragged sigh. His lips brushed her neck, and it arched for him instinctively. No, he told himself. Don't start what you can't finish.

An ache of longing racked his body, and he closed his eyes against it and swayed with her to the music, content for now just to hold her. Oh, his body wasn't content, but his head was, and it was his head he had to listen to.

He wasn't ready yet for more, and nor was she, at least not with him.

Not yet, and maybe not ever.

She'd had fun, more fun than she'd had for years, and in the way Owen had he'd made her feel really special, but inevitably it had to come to an end. He took her home at a little after one, because she had to open the shop next morning and she needed a few hours' sleep.

He pulled up outside, and Cait hesitated before opening the car door. 'Would you like a coffee?' she asked, but he shook his head.

'No. I don't think so. It's late, and you've got to get up.'

His hand reached out and cupped her cheek gently, and drew her towards him. 'Thank you for a wonderful evening,' he murmured softly, and then his lips claimed hers in a chaste, tender kiss that nevertheless made her bones melt and her breath jam in her throat.

Then, all too soon, he drew away and got out of the car, opening the door for her and seeing her in, brushing her lips one last time before he turned on his heel and walked back to the car.

She nearly ran after him, but her pride stopped her at the last moment, and instead she stood there on legs that seemed permanently useless these days and watched him go, then closed the door and locked it.

It had been a wonderful evening, he was right, and she hadn't wanted it to end. He had, though, or he would have taken her up on her offer of coffee. Perhaps it was just as well. It wasn't really coffee that she'd wanted, but just more time with him, and maybe that would have been too dangerous.

She went upstairs and found a message on the answering machine from Milly. She sounded puzzled that her mother had been out, and Cait sighed and took off the dress and hung it up. She'd get it dry-cleaned and put it back in stock—or maybe she'd keep it. She'd felt wonderful in it tonight, elegant and sexy and beautiful.

Yes, she'd keep it.

She looked at her watch. It was too late to ring Milly

now. She'd phone her in the morning. It didn't sound urgent, but the mother in her suffered a pang of guilt because she hadn't been there.

What if it had been urgent? What if Milly *had* needed her?

The phone rang, and she answered it instantly.

'I just wanted to say goodnight,' Owen said, his voice soft and slightly gruff. 'I didn't wake you, did I?'

'No—no, you didn't wake me, I haven't gone to bed yet. I missed a call from Milly,' she told him, and heard him sigh.

'I'm sorry. Was it urgent?'

'Didn't sound it, but you can't always tell. I don't know. Tell me I'm being silly.'

'I can't. I missed a call from Josh. I'll message him on his mobile—want me to message Emily?'

So that she knew her mother had been with Owen? Not likely! The inquisition would be unparalleled. 'Don't worry, I'll ring her tomorrow. Owen?'

'What?'

'Have you told Josh we've…seen each other?' she asked, not sure how to put it.

He sighed. 'No. I didn't know what to say, or even if there was anything to tell him. There hasn't been anyone since Jill—I don't know how he'll react. I'll tell him myself maybe, face to face. What about you? Have you told Milly?'

'No. I don't…have a social life. Well, not this sort, anyway,' she added, feeling the colour climb her cheeks.

'Cait, we haven't done anything wrong,' he said gently, and she sighed.

'I know. It's just—'

'I know. Don't worry—maybe we'll cross that bridge together later, if we get to that point. In the meantime, tell her something else—tell her you went to the super-market,' he suggested, and she laughed.

'It wouldn't be the first time,' she told him. 'Since it started opening twenty-four hours a day, I've often been in the middle of the night. It's sometimes the only time left. I just hate lying to her.'

'So tell her you went out with a friend. It's not so far from the truth, is it?'

He sounded almost wistful, and Cait smiled sadly. 'No. No, it's not far from the truth at all. I'll tell her that.'

'Good. And I'll see you tonight.'

'Tonight?' she echoed, her heart racing. He hadn't mentioned another date, and she'd been feeling a little rejected. How silly.

'Or tomorrow, whatever you want to call it. Saturday night. Wear something more casual, and don't eat. I'll see you at seven-thirty.'

'I'll look forward to it,' she said, wondering if he could hear the eagerness she knew must be in her voice. 'And…Owen?'

'Mmm?'

'Thank you for tonight.'

There was a tiny hesitation, then he said softly, 'You're welcome, sweetheart. It was my pleasure. See you soon. Sleep well.'

She replaced the phone regretfully, stripped off her make-up and climbed into bed in her serviceable old nightshirt. Her body was still humming from the contact with his as they'd danced, and just the memory made her ache for more.

He'd obviously been affected by their dance, too, and had been unable to disguise his reaction, but unlike the average man he'd made no move to pursue that interest or push her into anything she wasn't ready for.

Still, he'd proved over and over again that he was more than an average man, and he was a lot more mature than the last man to take an interest in her. Still, that had been fifteen or so years ago, and that thoroughly average experience had been enough to put her off for life.

Until Owen.

She wondered what he'd got planned for them that night. Goodness knows. He'd given her no clues on the phone, apart from telling her not to eat and to dress casually. Still, she didn't care. Just being with him was enough.

Cait snuggled down under the quilt, closed her eyes and fell instantly asleep, happier than she'd been for years.

CHAPTER SIX

'A PUB crawl!'

Owen laughed, his eyes crinkling with humour and his lips twitching. 'Yes, a pub crawl. Are you doing anything early tomorrow?'

Cait shook her head, wondering what was in store for her that he needed to ask that. 'No. Nothing—well, I was going to sort stock at some point. Why, won't I be well enough?'

He laughed again. 'Of course you will! I'm not going to get you legless, sweetheart. I was just going to suggest you bring some overnight things, then we can go by taxi and I can get in the spirit of it, too—or we can do that and I can get the taxi to run you back. It's up to you. No strings. I just thought it might be rather nice to have our own sleep-over party.'

She hesitated for a moment, troubled because she still hadn't been able to get hold of Milly on the phone, but then she surrendered with a smile. 'OK. I'll get some things together. Come on up—it's tidy for once. I cleaned up in your honour.'

'I'd better come and make it worthwhile, then, hadn't I?' he said with a grin, and followed her up the stairs.

She turned to him at the top. 'It's not like yours,' she warned him.

Owen caught her hands and held them lightly, staring down into her eyes, his face serious now. 'I didn't expect it to be, Cait. Stop worrying. You know I'm proud of all you've achieved. I'm not interested in judging you.'

She felt tears welling in her eyes, and turned away. 'Don't be silly. Come in.'

He followed her, looking round with interest. She'd thought he'd probably sit politely down, but he didn't. He prowled, fingering things, looking at her little treasures—clay models Milly had made at kindergarten, a framed Mother's Day card ditto, a funny little knitted cat that was meant to be Bagpuss.

He smiled indulgently as he examined them, and she could tell that he had a similar set of treasures collected over the years. He was a sentimental man, and she wondered how he had coped with Jill's death and if it still haunted him.

Certainly he still wore his wedding ring, and she wondered if he was ready for another relationship or if he really was just offering her friendship with no strings attached, just as he'd said.

'I won't be long. Sit down,' she suggested hopefully, but he just smiled and said he was all right and carried on prowling.

Cait came back a few minutes later after a hunt for a decent nightdress, to find him on the lumpy old sofa with Bagpuss shedding hair all over his dark trousers.

'Oh, no, look what's she's done!' she exclaimed, and handed Owen the clothes brush. There was no way she was brushing down his lap!

'OK?' he asked after a few vigorous strokes, and she nodded.

'You'll do. Sorry about that—you're a bad cat, Bagpuss! Come on, I'll feed you. You'd better have enough to last tomorrow morning, if Owen's going to lead me astray,' she said to the cat, who just purred and wound herself around Cait's legs.

Owen was chuckling.

'What?' she said.

'Me, leading you astray. As if I would,' he murmured, and winked at her.

She sighed inwardly. Unfortunately she didn't think there was the slightest chance of him leading her astray, despite the wink. He was far too much of a gentleman, and she had a sickening feeling that he wanted much less from her than she wanted to give.

But, then, she was a desperate, lonely old maid.

Not that she'd have to be desperate to take an interest in him. He was enough to tempt a saint, and she'd lost any right to that office years ago. Oh, rats.

'Right, I'm ready,' she said, throwing the cat an extra measure of dry food and making a friend for life of her.

She flicked off lights, left the landing light on and ran down the stairs with Owen following her, her overnight bag firmly in his hand after he'd removed it from her.

Ever the gentleman.

She shut the door from the stairwell to the shop, locked it and then set the shop alarm on the way out of the door.

'Is there any risk of a break-in?' he asked her, and she shrugged.

'I don't know. I didn't want to take any chances, so I tend to set the alarm if I'm out for a long time— although they say most burglaries happen when you've gone to fetch a child from school or nipped to the shop, don't they?'

'Something like that. We were burgled in town while

we were at home, for goodness' sake—just because we left the window open in the sitting room when we'd gone out into the garden. They came in through the bay window in full view of the street, and nobody saw a thing.'

She thought how she'd feel, and shuddered. 'It must have been awful. Did they take much?'

He gave a slow shake of his head. 'Not really. They broke something irreplaceable, though, a cup Josh had made for Jill at school. That was the worst thing. Nothing else seemed to matter by comparison.'

He opened the car door for her, and she looked up and caught a glimpse of pain in his eyes, and knew she'd been right. He was a man who valued little things, who knew the importance of tiny gestures and acts of kindness, and she felt her throat swell with emotion so that she could hardly swallow.

By the time he was behind the wheel she'd got herself together again, and he shot her a smile that didn't quite reach his eyes. 'OK?' he said, and she nodded, not quite able to trust her voice.

'Yes, I'm OK,' she managed after a moment, then changed the subject. 'So, where are we starting this pub crawl?' she asked brightly.

'Oh, in Audley. I've got a taxi coming for us at eight-fifteen.'

'Such extravagance,' she teased, and he shrugged.

'You could drive, if you like, but it rather defeats the object.'

'So it does,' she agreed. 'So, which pub first and why?'

'The Dirty Duck—they have a brilliant starter menu.'

'Starter menu?' she said, puzzled.

He shot her a grin. 'Oh, yes. You didn't think we were going to go to all these pubs and just drink, did you?'

She had—well, she'd imagined he'd told her not to

eat so he could feed her, not so she'd get drunk quicker, but she had no real idea what he'd got in mind.

It turned out to be a culinary guided tour. They had chopped mushrooms and smoky bacon on toast in the Dirty Duck, washed down with a glass of something delicious from their wine cellar, followed by a brisk walk across town to the Wagon and Horses for a wonderful pot roast with the most fabulous vegetables and a glass of vintage claret, then on to the Bell for the wickedest chocolate mousse she'd ever tasted in her life, sitting on a puddle of Grand Marnier and topped with the creamiest cream and a fanned strawberry garnish, with a glass of wonderfully mellow muscat to sip alongside it.

'That,' she told him as she scraped the last tiny bit of chocolate mousse from the dish and levelled her spoon at him, 'was not your average pub crawl.'

Owen chuckled. 'I thought you'd never been on one?' he said.

'That doesn't mean I don't know what they're like,' she pointed out, 'and that wasn't it.' She sat back, still licking her lips, and sighed hugely. 'That was...' She trailed to a halt, lost for words, and he gave a low chuckle.

'That good, eh?'

'Absolutely. Remind me never to cook for you—it's just underlined how useless I really am.'

He chuckled again and poured the last dribble of muscat into her glass. 'Come on, drink up, we've got to have the next course.'

Cait stared at him in open-mouthed amazement. 'Next course?' she squeaked, and he nodded.

'Yup—Irish coffee and after-dinner mints by the fire at my house. The taxi'll be outside in a moment. Are you ready?'

She nodded, a little dazed. 'Yes, I'm ready. I don't

know if I can stand, but I'm ready.' She smiled at him, wondering if she looked and sounded as merry as she felt, and remembered his promise not to get her legless.

Well, it wasn't exactly a promise, which was just as well since he probably had no idea what a cheap drunk she was. One sip and she was away usually, and tonight she'd had three glasses.

Oops.

Oh, well, in for a penny...

She drained her glass and stood up, managing not to fall over while he helped her into her coat, and then the taxi whisked them back out into the velvet darkness of the countryside and she leant on his arm in the back and sighed contentedly.

'OK?'

'Mmm.' She felt too lazy to speak, and didn't argue when he eased his arm out from behind her and wrapped it round her shoulders, shifting so that her head came to rest on his chest and her arm just naturally snuggled round his waist. 'Mmm,' she said again, and closed her eyes. It felt so good...

She was asleep by the time they got back to his house, and he woke her gently. 'Cait? We're back.'

She sat up sleepily, and he got out of the taxi and paid the driver, then went round and helped her out.

'Come on, sleepyhead,' he said gently, and she looked up at him as the clouds parted, her face silvered with moonlight, and smiled mistily.

'Sorry—I'm not used to drinking so much,' she told him, as if he hadn't already realised that. 'It just knocks me out.'

'You can't go to sleep yet, we've still got to have the coffee and liqueur phase of the meal,' he reminded her.

'Just coffee,' she told him, sounding just a fraction

tipsy, and he felt a twinge of guilt. Hopefully she wouldn't feel too hungover the next day.

'Come on,' he coaxed, and led her into the house and settled her in the corner of the settee nearest the fire.

The dogs greeted them with enthusiastic wagging, and he let them out for a run and gave them a biscuit while he made the coffee.

He passed on the Irish whiskey. Cait certainly didn't need it and he wasn't sure he did, either. The last thing he wanted was to drink so much that he woke up tomorrow not knowing what he'd done, if anything, and he needed all his wits about him with her looking so soft and warm and sleepy.

Owen sat down on the other side of the fireplace, well away from temptation, and pushed the coffee towards Cait across the low table.

'Hey, sleepyhead,' he said, and she cracked an eye open.

'You talking to me?' she asked, and he nodded.

'I am. Your coffee's there.'

'Laced?'

He shook his head. 'No. Not laced. I thought we'd probably both had enough.'

She sat forwards and kicked off her shoes, picked up her coffee and snuggled back into the corner with her feet tucked under her bottom and her nose buried in the mug.

'Mmm,' she said appreciatively, and he smiled and leant back, stretching out his legs in front of him and indulging his senses.

A warm fire, a comfortable chair, good coffee—and a beautiful woman to look at. What more could a man want?

To take her to bed and make long, slow, lazy love to her, he thought, and swore silently. Ain't ever gonna happen, he told himself. Down, boy. You promised.

He snagged a handful of chocolate mint sticks and

nudged the stereo remote control, and soft music poured over them, lazy and romantic. They stayed there like that for ages, long after the coffee was finished and the fire had died down and the CD had played out, and then he stood up and drew her to her feet.

'Come on, let's get you to bed. You look wiped.'

'You said you weren't going to get me legless,' she teased, and stumbled slightly against him.

'Hopeless creature. You didn't tell me you had no head at all for it.'

'Of course I haven't! I'll have you know I'm a model of propriety,' she said, and spoilt it by giggling.

Owen gave up. Scooping her into his arms, he carried her up the stairs and along the walkway to her room, then set her gently down on her feet in the doorway. Her bag was there, all ready for her, and he thought she could probably manage to get herself ready for bed. If she couldn't, well, she'd sleep as she was, because there was no way he trusted himself with her, not when she was so deliciously defenceless.

He reached out a hand and cupped Cait's cheek, and the moonlight streaming through the window beside him gleamed dully on the worn gold of his wedding ring.

He looked at it in surprise. He hadn't even thought about it for a while, but now it seemed out of place, somehow disloyal to both Jill and Cait. And if anything could have reminded him of his responsibilities, that was it.

He dropped his hand to his side and gave her a crooked smile.

'Goodnight, sweetheart,' he murmured. 'Sleep well.'

His lips brushed hers lightly, and he turned and left her standing there in the doorway. He closed his door firmly, sat down on the edge of the bed and picked up the photo of Jill that sat on the bedside table.

Odd, how he could hardly remember her now after all the time they'd been together. He could still hear her voice sometimes in things Josh said, but he found it increasingly hard to remember her face.

Four years, he thought. Just a short while, and yet it felt like a lifetime.

He could hear Cait moving around in her room at the other end of the walkway, and he wished it was a drawbridge that he could pull up, to keep them both safe from each other.

He put the photo of Jill back on the bedside table to watch over him and keep him in order, and then he took off his clothes, crawled under the quilt and lay listening to the small sounds from Cait's room until the house was quiet.

Then he fell into a restless sleep, and dreamed of her...

CHAPTER SEVEN

CAIT woke to sun streaming in and a pounding headache.

'Oh, no,' she groaned, and slid under the quilt, shutting out the light. Better, but not a lot. Oh, heck.

'Serves you right,' she told herself a while later when the little men had put their hammers down and seemed to be taking a tea-break. 'You know you can't drink.'

She heard a firm tread on the walkway and scraped up the mental energy to wonder just how much of a fright she looked. She'd taken her make-up off the night before, but without fail a trace of mascara would remain and work its way down her cheeks in the night, giving her panda eyes.

Her hair was on end, her head was thumping again and the last thing she wanted to do was put on a cheerful face. She decided not to bother. It was, after all, his fault.

After a gentle knock, Owen popped his head round the door. 'Hello, sleepyhead,' he said softly, and she twitched the quilt down and looked blearily at him across the room.

'Hello yourself,' she growled. 'You're looking disgustingly chipper.'

He smiled just a touch smugly. 'How's the head?'

'Grim. How's yours?'

'Fine,' he said, and finally had the grace to look apologetic. 'I've brought you tea, if you fancy it.'

Cait slid carefully up the bed, dragging the quilt after her, and tucked it firmly under her armpits. 'I always fancy tea,' she told him, and rested her head gently back against the high wooden headboard with a groan.

'Sit up,' he told her, and tucked another pillow behind her shoulders for her sore head to rest on. 'How's that?'

'Lovely,' she croaked, and reached for the tea. The mug arrived in her fingers, and she buried her nose in it and sipped cautiously. 'Oh, gorgeous,' she mumbled, and worked her way steadily down it.

By the time she'd finished the second cup, the little men were just tapping gently and she thought she might survive the day. Owen, bless his heart, was mercifully silent, just sitting by the window on a comfy chair sipping tea and staring out over the valley.

He looked across at her and smiled. 'Better?'

'Much, thank you,' she said with feeling. Putting the cup down, she snuggled the covers up round her shoulders and sighed. 'I can't believe I'm hungover,' she said disgustedly, and he chuckled.

'It was probably the muscat. It's wickedly strong.'

'It was perfect with the chocolate mousse—which incidentally had a good slug of liqueur in it. I forgot to count that.'

'Ah, yes, the chocolate mousse. I should have warned you. I've had it before—it's enough to put you over the limit without anything else, just about.'

'To be fair, I can get drunk on my neighbour's sherry-flavour trifle,' she said drily, and he chuckled again. She gave him a sour look. 'You're in a very good mood,' she said crossly.

One brow kicked up. 'Do I take it you aren't a morning person, sweetheart?' he said with an almost straight face, and she threw a pillow at him.

Owen caught it and threw it back, and she buried her face in it and rolled over onto her side, groaning. 'What time is it?' she asked through the pillow.

'If you just said what I think you did, it's eleven thirty.'

She dropped the pillow and sat up. 'What!' she squawked. 'It can't be!'

'It is. Why, should you be somewhere?'

Cait shook her head—not a wise move—and groaned.

'You need some breakfast and some fresh air, probably in the reverse order. Why don't you have a quick shower and we'll take the dogs for a little stroll down to the river, then come back and have a good hearty breakfast?'

'Go away,' she said very clearly, and fell back into the pillows with a groan.

He was utterly heartless, she decided later when she'd calmed down a bit. He smiled a barracuda smile, leant over and plucked the quilt off her in one easy movement, walking out of the room with it and dropping it over the banisters.

'I'll see you downstairs in five minutes,' he said, and she hurled a pillow at his head.

He ducked back out of the way, and she heard his chuckle echo down the stairs and into the kitchen.

Brute, she thought, lying back against the remaining pillow and wishing she could die. All the pillow-hurling had got the little men back from their tea-break, and she gave up the unequal struggle and slid off the bed, went into the bathroom and turned on the power shower and nearly blasted her skin off.

She felt better, irritatingly, but she had to concede the point. Maybe he'd be right about the fresh air and break-fast as well.

How sickening!

* * *

It was a beautiful day. They walked the dogs down through the fields and across the little bridge over the river, and then through the woods on the far side before coming back.

It was quiet and peaceful, with nothing to disturb them but the song of the birds and the rustle of squirrels in the trees. There was a stile to climb over, and Owen helped Cait down and then somehow forgot to let go of her so that they strolled back hand in hand, and she magnanimously forgave him for her hangover—even though it had really been her own fault.

'I'm sorry I was crabby,' she said as they got back to the house, and he turned her into his arms and kissed the tip of her nose and smiled.

'I forgive you. You were quite entertaining.'

She closed her eyes and counted to ten, but while they were shut he kissed her again, only on the lips this time, and she forgot to breathe—forgot everything, including how far out of her league he was and all the other reasons this might be a bad idea, and she went up on tiptoe and kissed him right back.

After a while he lifted his head and she sank down onto her heels again and rocked back and looked up at him, slightly dazed.

'Breakfast,' he said, his voice gruff, and she nodded and followed him in, her heart pounding.

Nobody had ever kissed her like that. Nobody. Ever. Not in thirty-five and a half years.

And all he could talk about was breakfast!

Owen took her back to her flat at three, and once again Milly had tried to phone—the night before, and twice during the morning.

'Get out of that,' she said with a sigh, and dropped into

the armchair by the phone. She punched in the number, crossed her fingers and forced a smile into her voice.

'Hi, darling, how are you?' she asked brightly.

'Worried to death. Where have you *been*?'

'Sorry, sweetheart, I should have told you. I went out for a drink last night and then we went back for coffee and it was late so I stayed over. What's the matter? Is anything wrong?'

'No,' Milly said slowly. Damn. Cait could hear the cogs working. 'Who were you out with?'

What now? A direct lie, or the truth, when Owen hadn't told Josh yet?

'Nobody you know,' she said noncommittally.

'A man? Hey, Ma, have you got a man, after all this time? Amazing! Tell me all! What's he like?'

'I didn't say it was a man.'

'You didn't have to. It's in your voice, you sound different.' A slight pause, then, 'Did you say you stayed over?'

Cait closed her eyes and prayed for the ground to open up. 'Nothing happened,' she said truthfully. 'I stayed in the spare room. Alone. All night.'

'Oh.' Silence while her daughter digested this, then with the resilience of youth she moved on. 'Anyway, why I was ringing was, there's this ball coming up—the Hall Freshers' Ball? It's next weekend, and I don't have a dress with me, and I don't suppose there's any way you could throw something together and send it down, is there?'

'What, post it?' she said, wondering what on earth it would cost and if it would arrive, but Milly was way ahead of her with it all worked out.

'No, not post it,' she said. 'Josh's dad is coming down next Friday for a conference. If I give you his address, you could let him have it, and he could bring it down!'

'Da-dah!'

Cait waited for a white rabbit to pop out of the end of the phone. So easy. Just make me a dress, give it to a man you don't know—hah—to bring me, and hey presto! Madam could go to the ball.

Never mind that her mother might not have time to do it!

'What sort of dress?' she asked, actually only too glad to get Milly permanently off the subject of her sleep-over party with Owen.

'Oh, you know—something a bit like that gold one but less bad.'

Cait nearly choked. 'The gold one?' she squeaked.

'Yes, you know, that strappy thing.'

Straps was all it was. It was the one Owen had jokingly pulled out, and there was no way her darling little daughter was going anywhere in a creation like that!

'I've sold it,' she lied, but Milly snorted.

'You just don't want me wearing a slapper's dress,' she retorted, hitting the nail on the head, and Cait sighed.

'Why on earth would you want to?' she asked with a touch of desperation. 'Anyway, I don't have time. How about a nice simple halter-neck dress with a pouffy underskirt and a stole? Or something slinky—a crêpe cut on the cross, or a shot-silk bodice and a black skirt? There are lots of them around this year—'

'Mum, you're boring! I'm not thirty! I want something young!'

'So go and buy one!' she suggested, but Milly sighed unhappily and so they started again, renegotiating until they came to some kind of compromise.

'So, when will you start it?' she asked, and Cait rolled her eyes.

'I'll look through my fabric stocks now. I'm sure

I've got something that will do. I just hope it fits, because there's nothing I can do about it if it doesn't.'

'It'll fit,' her daughter said with confidence, and Cait hoped she was right. Still, she could set up the model to Milly's size, which would help.

'OK, darling, I'll see what I can do.'

'Right—and, Ma? You have fun, OK? You deserve it. You've given up enough for me. It's time you had some fun. Go for it.'

Oh, lord. Cait felt her heart rising up in her throat and threatening to choke her. 'Thanks, darling,' she said unsteadily, and after a few maternal warnings about sex and drugs and alcohol and not working hard enough, she put down the phone and sat back, her mind whirling.

Go for it?

Really?

Still, why not? As Milly had pointed out, she'd given up enough. It was time for her—and she ought to take advantage of every opportunity.

Carpe diem—seize the day.

'Absolutely,' she said with resolution. 'By the scruff of the neck—if I can find the courage.'

'I gather I'm conveying a ball gown to London on Friday when I go down for this conference,' Owen said on the phone later.

'If I can make it in time. I've got so much to do—including another Law essay for tomorrow night.'

'You're nuts,' he told her, for the third or fourth time. 'Anyway, what sort of dress? Haven't you got one in stock that would do?'

'Oh, yes. I've got one she wants, but she's not having it. That gold one you pulled out,' she told him, and he nearly choked down the phone.

'Good grief! Can this be your daughter?'

'I don't know,' Cait said worriedly. 'I'm just beginning to wonder that myself. The worrying thing is, maybe she's more like her mother than is good for her.'

'Oh, come on, now, don't be hard on yourself because you made a mistake when you were a kid,' he said softly, and she sighed.

'I'll die if she throws her life away like I did.'

'You didn't throw it away,' he corrected. 'You spent it doing something wonderful—you gave Milly her life. Don't underrate that.'

'And she's just told me I've wasted enough of my life and I should go for it.'

'Go for what?' he asked, sounding puzzled, and she told him about the conversation she'd had with her daughter about her whereabouts the night before.

Owen laughed without humour. 'I haven't told Josh. I don't have your courage.'

'I didn't *tell* Milly,' she said drily. 'She guessed. She said I sounded different. I don't know if she believed me when I said nothing happened. I just felt sick telling her. I'm so afraid she'll judge me.'

'Don't be afraid,' he murmured. 'She won't—and even if she does in the short term, at the end of the day she'll realise all you've done for her and she'll come round. They need to grow up before they can deal with complex adult emotions.'

They're not alone, Cait thought as she struggled to rough out a design for Milly's dress that evening. She was dealing with some pretty complex emotions herself, and she was way out of her depth.

She loved Owen, of that she was sure. Whether he loved her or not was highly debatable. If he did—or even, come to that, if he didn't—why hadn't he made love to her last night? Heaven knows, she was more than willing, and she wouldn't have put up much of a fight.

Perhaps that was the trouble. Maybe he liked his women sober and co-operative, not falling asleep and stumbling drunkenly around. She just hoped she hadn't disgraced herself. She didn't think she had, but her judgement was a bit iffy and her memory was probably not entirely accurate.

'Never again,' she mumbled through a mouthful of pins, and stood back to look at her mock-up.

It would do fine, she thought. A little tuck here, perhaps—yes, that was better. She rummaged through her fabrics, found something black and electric blue in a striking shot silk effect that would look stunning on her dark-haired daughter, and by the time she went to bed she'd put it together and hung it on the model to drop, so she could hem it the next day.

Success. All she had to do now was her Law essay!

'So this is it, then?'

'Yes. Try not to crease it—even though she'll throw it on the floor once she's worn it, and I expect someone will spill something down it within the first five minutes.'

'Or worse. Half of them had alcohol poisoning after Saturday night, apparently,' he told her.

'I am not going to presume to criticise,' Cait said piously, and he laughed.

'You were a very long way off alcohol poisoning.'

'It didn't feel like that on Sunday morning.'

'You were fine. You were just a bit tiddly. I'm still feeling guilty.'

'Good,' she said, firmly squashing her smile. 'When will you be back from London?'

'Oh, late,' Owen said with a sigh. 'Friday night traffic is hideous. I thought I might avoid it and take Josh out for dinner. He said I could doss on his bed and he'll sleep on the floor, but I think I need my creature comforts and, anyway, I have to get back for the dogs—unless you want to sleep there for me?'

'I have to open the shop on Saturday,' she reminded him, and he nodded.

'That's fine. I'll come back tomorrow night late. Mrs Poole can go in and feed them at five, and they'll be fine till I get home.'

'Ring me when you get back—tell me how she looks,' she said, and wondered if her voice was really as mournful as it seemed to her.

'She'll be fine. I might be very late.'

'Still, please, ring. I want to know you're safely home.'

His eyes flickered with something she couldn't quite read, and he put the dress down carefully and drew her into his arms.

'I have to go now,' he said, cradling her against his body. 'I've got work to do before I can leave tomorrow.'

'I might do my next Law assignment so I don't have to stay up all Sunday night again,' she mumbled into his shirt, and then she breathed in deeply and sighed with contentment. He smelt warm and familiar and absolutely right, a combination of soap and man that was utterly intoxicating.

Maybe that was what had pushed her over the edge on Saturday?

Owen lifted his head and smiled at her tenderly. 'I have to go.'

She nodded, and went up on tiptoe to kiss him goodbye. 'Don't forget the dress,' she reminded him, 'or Cinderella won't be going to the ball.'

'Cinderella? Milly? Not a chance. By all accounts she hasn't missed a single evening out—unlike her mother.'

'Oh, her mother's fine. Although…' Cait tipped her head on one side and looked up at him with an ironic smile '…you know something? You know what I do for a living? I make and hire out ball gowns. And do you know I have never once, in my entire life, been to a ball? Isn't that the silliest thing you ever heard?'

He gave a slow, lazy smile, and pulled something from his pocket. 'That's just about to change,' he told her. 'Saturday week—in Audley. It's a fundraiser for the League of Friends of the hospital. I bought two tickets. So, *Cinderella*, you shall go to the ball!'

CHAPTER EIGHT

'YOU'VE taken your wedding ring off.'

Owen glanced down at his finger, still strangely bare and feeling very naked, and nodded.

'Yes, I have.'

'Have you got a woman?'

He looked at his son, trying to read his feelings and failing hopelessly. 'I have met someone, yes.'

Josh looked away, his eyes veiled. 'I wondered if you would, when I went away.'

'It wasn't planned.'

The boy shrugged, and Owen got the distinct impression he was trying to hide his hurt.

'Josh, it's just coincidence. I didn't deliberately go out of my way to find someone the moment you were gone, but I met her, and the time seemed right.'

'Are you sleeping together?'

He felt the shock of the question right down to his toes, and almost glanced over his shoulder to see if anyone else in the crowded restaurant had heard. It seemed unlikely.

'Not that I think it's any of your business,' he said in a low voice, 'but, no, I'm not. Not yet, at least.'

'But you might.'

'I might.'

Josh speared him with a penetrating stare. 'Would Mum approve of her?'

He thought of Jill and Cait, so different and yet in many ways so similar, and he nodded slowly. 'Yes, I think so.'

'That's all right, then. Just so long as you're happy.'

'I am,' Owen said, and realised as he spoke that it was true. 'I'm happier than I've been for years.'

'Good.' Josh changed the subject, obviously uncomfortable with it, and Owen eased out a sigh of relief and settled down to listen to the catalogue of wild parties and endless shenanigans the freshers had got up to since they'd last spoken.

Good grief, he thought, Cait and I are going to have to get a great deal wilder to compete with that lot!

'Just don't spend *all* your money on alcohol,' he cautioned, which was a rash thing to do, because he ended up shelling out for a set of textbooks that cost more than he would have believed possible.

Ah, well, he thought, it's only money. And then he wondered how Cait would provide for Milly, and thought again just how much she'd sacrificed to give the girl her chance in life.

Suddenly he couldn't wait to get back to her.

'Will I do?'

Cait twirled in front of him, the new gown she'd just completed swirling out around her and settling back with a silken whisper against her skin.

It was a wonderful deep sapphire colour, perfect with her colouring, and it made her skin look like alabaster. Owen felt his body surge to life, and cleared his throat.

'You look lovely,' he said, his voice sounding strained to his ears, and she smiled diffidently and coloured, a soft wash of pale rose tinting her skin and bringing her to life. Lord, she was gorgeous. He hardly dared trust himself to touch her, but he helped her into her coat with fingers that trembled to caress her skin, and when he brushed her shoulder accidentally with the back of his hand, heat shot through him.

'I've got my overnight things,' she said, and he nodded curtly.

'Fine. Let's go, then. The taxi's picking us up from home in fifteen minutes.'

He hardly had time to put her bag in the spare room before the taxi beeped outside, and he ran down, patted the dogs absently and ushered her out.

It was a clear night, crisp and cold, and he knew it would freeze later. He'd lit the fire—partly for the dogs, and partly so they would have a focus of warmth when they came back so they could sit up and drink coffee and talk into the wee small hours of the night.

He wasn't thinking beyond that, wasn't letting his mind or his imagination run away with him. He didn't dare. One thing at a time, he told himself. One thing at a time.

The ball was everything Cait might have hoped for and more. Everyone was elegantly turned out, and she recognised some of her dresses in the crowd.

While Owen was getting them drinks, one of her regulars saw her and did a mild double take. 'Cait?' she said, and smiled a broad welcome. 'We don't usually see you at these things! How nice to see you on the other side of the counter, as it were. What a gorgeous dress!'

She turned to the tall and rather striking man beside her. 'Darling, this is Cait Cooper—she's got that wonderful ball gown hire shop in Wenham, and she makes the most fabulous dresses. She's amazing. Oh, that sounds so patronising, but it isn't meant to be, Cait. You really are so talented. I can't believe how lucky we are to have you.'

'Aren't we?' Owen said, coming up behind her. 'Cait, allow me to introduce you to Ryan and Ginny O'Connor. By the sound of it you've met Ginny before, and Ryan's someone I hope you'll never meet professionally—he's one of our A and E consultants.'

'Ah! Right. Hi, there,' she said, laughing softly at Owen's introduction and shaking Ryan's hand. 'It's nice to meet you. I hardly ever get to meet the husbands.'

'They're cheated,' he said gallantly in a soft Canadian burr, and he winked at her. 'I shall have to make a point of coming along for fittings in future.'

'If you're allowed,' Ginny retorted. 'It's a girly thing, usually, isn't it, Cait?'

'Only because men get bored to death. They just don't have our stamina.'

'You can say that again,' Ryan groaned. He slid an arm round his wife's waist and drew her closer. 'How about that dance you promised me?' he murmured, and Ginny smiled at Cait and Owen and excused herself, and they went off towards the dance floor.

Cait's eyes followed them longingly. She'd never danced anywhere except at a nightclub or a disco, and that only a very few times in her life. Certainly she'd never danced in a long, floaty dress with a man's arms around her as he whirled her round the floor.

'Sounds like a good idea.' Owen's voice was soft, his breath teasing her skin. He was still standing slightly behind her, and his hands came up and cupped her shoulders, bringing a shiver of anticipation to her skin. 'What do you think?'

'I think it sounds like a lovely idea,' she said a trifle breathlessly, and turned towards him. 'Could we?'

Heavens, was she really as wistful as she sounded? Owen's eyes creased in a smile. 'I'm sure we could.' He cupped her elbow with his hand and led her to the dance floor, then turned her into his arms.

'I don't think I can remember any of the fancy things,' she told him, and he chuckled.

'I never knew them. Just relax. I won't know if you do it wrong, and if you're very careful I probably won't tread on you more than a few times.'

He didn't tread on her at all, and Cait was sure he was lying about not knowing the steps. She didn't care. She just rested one hand on his shoulder, placed her other hand in his and let him guide her. At first he kept a discreet distance between them, but gradually they settled closer together, until her head was on his shoulder and their clasped hands were tucked in against their bodies, so that the back of his hand brushed her breast.

She could feel the shift of his thighs against hers as they moved slowly to the music, and after a while her steadily building awareness threatened to consume her. To an outsider they would have appeared just like any other couple dancing, she thought, and yet she could feel the tension humming in him, the savagely suppressed passion simmering just below the surface, like a banked furnace.

Finally the master of ceremonies called the last dance, and she could feel the tension in him mounting to unbearable levels. Then the music swirled to a halt with a flourish, the band were sent off to thunderous applause and Owen eased away from her and looked down into her eyes.

'Time to go,' he said gruffly, and she could see the desire burning in his eyes.

They were silent in the taxi, and when they arrived back at the house he put the dogs out, then filled the kettle and put it on the Aga.

'Coffee?' he asked, and Cait lifted her shoulders in a tiny shrug.

'If you want.'

Their eyes met and locked. 'You know what I want,' he said, his voice low and taut with emotion.

She smiled a little unsteadily. 'So what are you waiting for, Owen?' she murmured.

He closed his eyes briefly and then opened them again, and she almost staggered under the force of the need that blazed from them. 'Dogs,' he said distractedly, and went to the back door, calling them in.

He threw them a biscuit each, took the kettle off the hob and held out his hand. 'Come to bed,' he said softly, and her legs nearly gave way.

Reaching out her hand, she placed it in his, her trust in him absolute. She had never loved like this before, and she knew she never would again. As her hand linked with his, so did her heart and soul, and in that moment she gave herself to him completely.

The sun streaming in through the window woke Owen, and he propped himself up on one elbow and looked down at Cait. She was beautiful—her skin warm and flushed with sleep, her lashes like dark crescents against her rose-petal cheeks.

Her lips were slightly swollen from their kisses, and there was a touch of whisker-burn on her lip. He leant over and kissed it better, and her lashes fluttered up and she smiled at him.

'Hi,' she said, her voice shy and tentative, and he smiled back and kissed her again.

'Hi yourself. How are you?'

'Wonderful,' she told him, her eyes shining. 'How are you?'

'Likewise.' He eased the quilt away from her shoulders and looked down at her, at the soft dusky rose of her nipples puckering in the cool air, the smooth swell of her breasts, the flat plain of her stomach. She was beautiful, and he felt desire rip through him again.

He'd been right when he'd thought she'd be amazing to make love to. Her face was a mirror of her feelings, every touch, every stroke of his hands registering in her expressive features.

He kissed her again, and she reached for him, drawing him into her arms, and he was lost.

Cait had never been so happy. She'd thought she'd known what to expect, but afterwards she realised that her slight and very limited experience hadn't prepared her at all for the love-making of a skilled and patient man. Every touch had registered, every kiss had found its target, and when he took her home on Sunday night, she felt more cherished and loved than she'd ever felt in her entire life.

Nevertheless, at the back of her mind she worried that they hadn't taken any precautions, and so on Monday morning she went to see Max Carter, her GP.

'I don't think there's the slightest danger that I'm pregnant,' she told him frankly, 'because it's right at the end of my cycle, but I ought to go on the Pill for the future, I think.'

He nodded. 'I can give you a prescription for the morning-after pill as it's called, if you like, but you don't sound as if you think it's necessary, and it's getting a bit late now for it to be effective anyway. It's up to you.'

She shook her head. 'No. I'm sure I'm safe. I'm as regular as clockwork. I know I can't be pregnant.'

So he checked her over and gave her a prescription for the Pill, and she started taking it straight away to give her cover immediately after her period was over.

Except that it didn't come. The week passed, and Milly came home for the weekend and slept for most of it because she was so exhausted, and Cait cooked for her and tried not to think about what was happening inside her.

Perhaps it was because of the Pill, she thought, and ignored the nagging doubt. Not that she needed to be on the Pill, as it turned out, because she hardly saw Owen.

First, Milly and Josh were both up for the weekend, and then he had to go away to a conference, but she didn't really have time to miss him because she was into a frenzy with the Christmas ball rush starting and everyone panicking about their dresses.

He spoke to her on the phone from Italy, though, almost every day, and because she was so busy trying to ignore the time bomb that was going off inside her, she told him all about her Law course and how well it was going, and how she planned another course for the following year—maybe a residential course for a few weeks at a quiet time of the year, if she could afford it.

'That's great,' he said, sounding quite enthusiastic, and she thought, Oh, lord, he doesn't care if I go away. I wonder what he's doing in Italy, and with whom?

She threw herself back into the ball gowns, ignoring Owen and her missing period and her sudden loss of interest in tea and coffee.

Then finally she could ignore it no longer, because she woke up on the Tuesday morning just over two weeks after the ball, went into the bathroom with a pregnancy test kit and came face to face with her worst nightmare.

'You idiot!' she berated herself, tears streaming down her face. 'How could you have been such a fool? Twice, for goodness' sake!'

She thought of Emily, of the struggle she'd had to bring her up, the endless nights walking the floor with her and then trying to work during the day while her daughter slept; she remembered their flat, cold in winter and hot in summer and damp all year round, and she wrapped her arms round her waist and rocked her baby and sobbed as if her heart would break, because she loved its father and he didn't love her, and there was no way she could do anything but have it, and she was going right back to square one, her life in tatters all over again.

She went out of the bathroom and picked up the phone, staring at it blankly. Owen had rung at three o'clock in the morning to say he was back from his conference in Italy, and he wanted to see her again that night. Good, because she needed to see him, and suddenly she couldn't wait till the end of the day. She punched in his number, and he answered on the third ring, sounding sleepy and sexy and wonderful.

Except that he thought it was a good idea for her to go away on a Law course for a few weeks or months or whatever.

Oh, lord.

'I need to see you,' she said, her hand trembling. The little indicator strip was mocking her, and she put it down before she dropped it. 'Can I come round now?'

'Now?' he said, and she could hear the bedclothes rustling. 'Um—sure. Just give me half an hour to shower and dress.'

She couldn't wait that long. She got into her car, drove round to his house and sat outside, twisting her hands on the steering wheel until he opened the door and came out.

Her courage deserted her, and she sat there watching him as he crossed the gravel drive and pulled open her door, hunkering down beside her and taking her hands in his, his face worried.

'Cait?' he said softly. 'Darling, what's the matter? Is it Milly?'

She dragged in a shuddering breath. 'I need to talk to you.'

He straightened up, still holding her hand, and helped her out of the car. 'Come inside,' he said gently, and led her in, closing the door behind her and turning her into his arms.

She stood stiffly, her body frozen with shock and dread and the terrible acceptance of defeat, because she knew she was going to lose him, and she couldn't make her mouth say the words that would take him away from her for ever.

After a moment he dropped his arms and stepped back, looking down at her with his hands on her shoulders, steadying her as one shudder after another ripped through her frame.

'Cait, for God's sake, talk to me,' he said unsteadily, his voice ragged. 'What's wrong with you? What is it? Oh, God, tell me you're not dying.'

'Dying?' she said, freed suddenly from the immobility that had gripped her for the past few minutes. 'No, I'm not dying, Owen,' she said hollowly. 'I'm pregnant.'

CHAPTER NINE

'PREGNANT?'

Owen's hands fell to his sides, and he stabbed his fingers through his hair. His hand was trembling, Cait noticed absently, and any moment now he'd tell her she was trying to trick him into supporting her, and throw her out, as Robert and his father had done. She steeled herself for the blow—but it didn't fall.

Not yet, at least.

Finally he moved. 'Come and sit down,' he said gently, and led her through to the sitting room. 'Tea? Coffee?'

She shook her head, a shudder of distaste rippling through her. 'No, please. Nothing.'

She stood there, and he took her shoulders and pressed softly on them until her knees gave way and she sat down on one end of the sofa with a plop, then he sat at the other end, one leg hitched up, his elbow propped on the back, his head supported on his hand, watching her.

'I take it this isn't good news?' he said eventually, and she stared at him as if he were mad.

'Good news?' She laughed, and her voice cracked. 'How can it be good news?' she asked, close to hysteria. 'I've only just got Emily off my hands, I was just about to start my life! I'm thirty-five, Owen. I'll be fifty-three by the time this baby leaves for university—no, fifty-four! That's ancient! That's almost all my working life! I was going to have a career...'

Cait put down the hem of her sweater before she tore it in half, and bit her knuckle instead.

'Doing Law,' he said flatly.

'Something to do with it, probably.'

'Why?'

'Why?' She looked at him as if he had two heads. 'Because I've always wanted to do Law!'

'OK, so you want to do Law. What about your shop?'

She shrugged. 'I don't know. I can't afford to give it up, not for years, probably. I might have to pay for help so I can study.'

Owen nodded. 'And where does the baby fit into all this?'

She rolled her eyes. 'It doesn't! That's the whole *point*! The baby is just—I can't believe I was that stupid. All these years I've waited for my freedom, and the first half-decent man to come along and I throw it all away.'

'Was that supposed to be a compliment?' he interrupted, and his smile was strained.

She closed her eyes, the fight going out of her. 'I'm sorry. I didn't mean it like that. You've been wonderful to me, and it's been the best time of my life, but now I'm going to have to pay for it, like I always have to pay, and it's just so damned unfair.'

'Don't do anything silly, will you?' he said carefully, and there was an edge in his voice that made her look at him more closely.

'Silly? You mean have an abortion? You think that's what this is all about?'

'I don't know,' he said quietly. 'I hope not. If it is, then if there's anything I can do to change your mind—

I'll have the baby when it's born, bring it up, look after it, pay all its expenses—anything you want, Cait. Just don't kill my baby, please. I'll do anything rather than stand back and let you do that.'

Anything except marry me, she thought hollowly. Tell me you love me, Owen. Tell me you're overjoyed. Tell me anything, just don't sit there and be so bloody reasonable and try and negotiate.

'I don't want anything from you,' she lied. 'You can have access, of course you can, and see it as much as you want, but I don't want your money.' Just your heart.

'Can I see it every day? Every night?'

She stared at him, puzzled. 'Every day?'

'Yes. You said I could see it as much as I wanted. That's every day, Cait. I want to see my baby born. I want to see it grow up. I want to be there when it takes its first step, and kiss it better when it falls down. I'm not going to be an absentee father—not unless you make me.'

Owen reached out, taking her cold and lifeless hand in his warm, strong, vital one. 'Marry me, Cait,' he said, his voice vibrating with emotion. 'Marry me and live here with me and our baby. Be a family.'

It was such a wonderful thought that she nearly agreed, but then she remembered how he'd encouraged her to go away on the residential course she'd talked about, almost as if she'd become too much of a fixture in his life.

And the last thing she wanted was to be a burden to him, a duty, so she and her child became a sea-anchor weighing him down and ruining his life so that he ended up hating them both.

'You don't mean that. You're only saying it because you're afraid I'll kill it.'

'No.'

'Yes.' Cait dredged up a smile. 'It's all right, Owen, I'm not going to do anything stupid. You don't have to do the decent thing, as they say. I'm only telling you because I think you have a right to know.'

'So you won't marry me?'

She shook her head. 'It wouldn't work.'

'It might.' He glanced at his watch, then stood up. 'Look, I'm sorry, I have to go to the hospital. They rang just after you did and they've got a crisis on. I can't get out of it, or I would, because we have to talk this through. I'll come and see you tonight as soon as I get away, and in the meantime think about it. Think about the advantages and disadvantages of marrying me, and we'll talk again tonight. OK?'

She stood up. 'I won't change my mind, Owen,' she warned, and he gave her a grim little smile.

'Just take the time. Please. That's all I ask. Take the time, think about it and let me know your answer.'

She nodded in the end, because it was the easiest thing to do, and then she went home, opened up the shop and sat down at the desk with a piece of paper.

She wrote at the top 'Advantages' and 'Disadvantages', then wrote down all the pros and cons in the two columns.

At the end of the exercise one thing was clear. The advantages outweighed the disadvantages by about a hundred to one, but the one disadvantage was too huge to overcome.

'He'll hate me,' she'd written in shaky script, and even as she read it, her eyes filled and welled over, and she laid her head down on the desk and wept.

'Cait? Oh, dear, love, what's the matter?'

She dragged in a deep breath and sat up, scrubbing the tears from her cheeks. The lady who ran the antique shop next door was hovering by her desk, her eyes concerned. Cait dredged up a smile. 'Oh, hello, Gilda. I'm sorry, I was just having a wallow.'

'Oh, Cait. Missing Milly, I expect, are you? I remember when mine went away—awful. Just awful.'

Cait sniffed and nodded. She couldn't tell Gilda what was wrong—not now, before she'd got all her ducks in a row and decided what she was doing.

Although only an idiot would turn Owen down.

'Oh! You're not wearing it!'

'What?' She blinked at Gilda, who was staring dumbstruck at her hand. 'Wearing what?'

'Um—oh, nothing. A—a dress I thought you were wearing today, but you're not. I've just realised— Cait, I have to go, love. I just saw you through the window, and—well, take care. Come and have a chat if you want.'

Gilda patted her awkwardly on the shoulder and almost ran out, leaving Cait totally confused. What on earth was she on about?

She looked at her clothes, a plain pencil skirt and a neat blouse, with a comfy old cardigan snuggled over the top because the shop was always chilly until the sun came round, and shook her head. Gilda had really lost it.

She looked back down at her list, splodged with tears, and felt a sob welling in her chest. What on earth was she to do? Marry him, even though he was only doing it for the baby, or struggle on alone sharing her—or him—with Owen, scrapping about Christmas and birthdays and school holidays, with the poor little mite being passed from pillar to post?

At least Milly had had absolute security. They may have had nothing else, but her daughter had always known her mother would be there for her come hell or high water, at any hour of the day or night, and there had never been any question of how much she loved her.

'Oh, damn,' she said, and shut the list into her desk drawer. She had too much to do to waste time in useless contemplation. She'd talk to Owen tonight and, depending on what he said, she'd make a decision.

And, please, God, she thought, let it be the right one…

Owen struggled through a difficult day with an enormous effort of will. He was tired after the conference, suffering from lack of sleep, and standing in a hot theatre all day battling to save one life after another after a major incident was not his idea of a restful first day back.

Still, it occupied his mind totally, which was what he needed in the absence of being able to go and deal with his dilemma immediately.

Dilemma? he thought, and shook his head. No, not a dilemma. Well, not the baby, anyway. That wasn't a dilemma, it was a wonderful and precious gift, something he'd thought would never happen to him again. After Josh, he and Jill had never taken steps to prevent another pregnancy, but nothing had happened.

Jill hadn't really minded, but Owen had ached for another child for years, and it had only been when Jill had died that he'd finally resigned himself.

And now Cait was having his baby, and because she'd convinced herself she wanted to do something with Law, of all the dry and tedious things to want to study, she was seeing this precious gift of their child as a burden.

Well, he'd have to find a way to persuade her otherwise, so he could keep her safe and love and cherish her and their child till the end of his days.

If the stubborn, silly woman would only let him.

'Retractors,' he snapped, and the scrub nurse beside

him gave him a long-suffering look and slapped them in his hand. 'Sorry,' he mumbled, and her eyebrows shot up.

'You're like a bear with a sore head today,' she said under her breath. 'If I were you, I'd have a hot toddy and an early night.'

He snorted softly. If only it were that simple.

Owen rang Cait at six to say he was back at home and would like to see her.

She looked around her flat, horribly untidy because she'd been working late every night this week and had hardly given it a glance, and wanted to weep with frustration. At the very least, she wanted to have the place clean and tidy so he didn't start accusing her of being a slut and an unfit mother.

'I thought,' he went on, 'if you don't mind and haven't got any other plans, maybe I could get a taxi to pick you up and bring you here for a meal.'

So she was off the hook as far as the housework went, anyway. 'I don't know if I can eat,' she said worriedly, nausea nibbling at her even as she spoke.

'Don't worry about eating. You can have something simple. I just—Cait, give me a chance,' he said softly, and if she hadn't known better, she would have thought he really cared.

'I'll drive over,' she said.

'You don't need to do that,' he protested, but she cut him off.

'Yes, I do,' she corrected. 'I'm all right to drive. I'm pregnant, Owen, not crippled. I'll see you later. What time?'

'Seven?'

She looked at her watch and sighed. 'OK. I'll see you then.'

Pride made her dress up. Pride and a perverse urge to make him want her, even though she knew he didn't, not really. He was still in love with his wife, and she'd been a fool to imagine that she could have a part in his life.

She wore the black dress he'd liked the first time they'd gone out, even though it was ridiculously over the top for the occasion, and she put on slinky tights and high, strappy sandals that were totally impractical to drive in but made her legs look as if they went on for ever.

As an afterthought she put down extra food for Bagpuss, who was getting fat and bossy and more demanding than ever now Milly was gone, and she put on her best coat, courtesy of the Oxfam shop, and drove over to Owen's, arriving just a few seconds after seven.

He opened the door immediately and came over to the car to help her out. He was dressed in casual trousers and a cream cashmere sweater that set off his wonderful toffee-coloured eyes, and he scanned her with them as she stepped out of the car and for the briefest moment heat flared in them.

Good, she thought. She felt more confident knowing she still had some power over him, because she felt terrifyingly powerless in this situation. Not that it was about power, but the balance was firmly in his favour, and whatever happened she was going to be the loser once again.

Her hand slid down over her abdomen. No, not the loser, she thought. Never that, my little one. Not with you.

Owen took her elbow and helped her across the gravel, and because she was wearing those ridiculous shoes she let him. She got a stone in the toe, but she said nothing, just pasted on a smile and kept walking, and he took her into the house and settled her in the sitting room.

The fire was lit, and the dogs wagged their tails but

didn't bother to move. It was too warm and comfortable, and she didn't blame them.

'Can I get you a drink?'

Cait looked up into his eyes, shadowed now because his back was to the light, and wished she could read his expression. 'Please. Could I have water?'

'I've got mineral water—fizzy, with ice and lemon?'

It sounded wonderful. 'Please.'

He went up to the kitchen, and she surreptitiously slipped her shoe off and removed the stone, then put it back on just as he returned with a tall glass in each hand.

'How was work?' she asked, throwing him, and he gave a short laugh and dropped onto the other end of the sofa.

'Horrendous. There was a gas explosion in a factory. That's why they called me in. I spent the day gluing people together again, not always successfully.'

'I'm sorry.'

'Mmm. Whatever.' He stared down into his glass, shadows chasing across his face, and she knew he was reliving the horrors of the day. Then he turned to her, his eyes searching her face, and his mouth twitched into a fleeting smile. 'Sorry. I haven't even asked about you. How are you? How was your day? Are you OK?'

'Sick. Busy.' Sad because you don't love me.

'I'm sorry—about the baby. I feel so guilty about this, because I should really have thought about it when we made love, but—well, Jill and I never needed to. After Josh she didn't get pregnant again, and I suppose I've just stopped thinking about it.'

'Most woman are on the Pill,' she said in mitigation. 'You'd think I'd remember, but I didn't even think about it. I suppose it's been such a long time—it isn't something I do,' she explained, wondering if it was possible to become a virgin again after eighteen years, because that was what she'd felt like.

'No—I don't, either. It was the first time since Jill died. It just didn't seem right before, but somehow, with you—' He broke off, staring down into his glass again, and she wondered if he had a script concealed in it, little flashcards with key words on.

Oh, lord.

'I wasn't expecting it to be so beautiful,' he said softly, and his words nearly reduced her to tears. 'I thought it would be messy and difficult and I'd feel bad afterwards, but it wasn't and I didn't, and if we had to conceive a child, then to have done it that night seems somehow right.'

He put his glass down and took hers away, moving closer to her and taking her hand in his.

'Cait, I know this isn't what you wanted from your life, but it's happening, and we have to make the best of it. I don't know what you want to do, but if there's any way I can help, I will. If you want to go away and take a degree, I'll get a nanny to look after the baby and you can come home at weekends and in the holidays, and we'll manage somehow, if it's what you want.

'Or if you just want to carry on running your shop, you could let the flat and run it from here, or expand it upstairs into the flat, or move to another shop nearer—whatever. And Milly—there'll always be room for Milly here with you, you know that, don't you? Or if you just want to stop work and stay at home with the baby—whatever you want, whatever would make you happy.'

Owen trailed off, and she realised his eyes were glazed with tears. Oh, lord, she thought, he really wants this baby. If he and Jill never had any more and he wanted them, no wonder he's so desperate to have it here.

'You could even have the spare room, if you'd rather. We could divide off one end of it to make a nursery, and you and the baby could share it. Or you could have Josh's rooms and be even more separate, if you would rather.'

'What do you want?' she asked. 'Apart from the baby?'

'You,' he said after a long pause. 'I want you, Cait. I love you. I was going to ask you to marry me tonight, when I came back from Italy. I'd got a ring and everything. Then you started talking about going away, and I suddenly wasn't sure if you would want me.'

His voice cracked slightly, and Cait felt a great well of love building up inside her. 'Owen, of course I want you!' she said raggedly. 'I don't care about my course! It's boring. I just thought—I don't know, I'd thought about it for such a long time, and there it was. I was only doing it because I'd been planning it for years, but I don't want to go away. I don't want to do anything except have your baby and live here with you. I just didn't think you'd want me.'

'Not want you?' he said, stunned. 'Cait, how could I not want you? You're warm and funny and brave and beautiful—what is there about you not to want?'

'I can't cook,' she said, laughing tearfully. 'And I'm a lousy housewife.'

'That's fine. So am I. I have a housekeeper for that very reason.'

'And I'm an unmarried mother, and in your position in the community—'

'What position?' he said, his voice disgusted. 'People don't care about that sort of thing any more. Anyway, if I have anything to say about it you won't be an unmarried mother for very much longer.'

He slipped his hand into his pocket and pulled out a little ring, diamonds and sapphires in a very old setting, the light sparkling off the stones and dazzling her through her tears. 'I got it from Gilda next door. I told her it was for you. I didn't tell her why, but I think she guessed.'

Cait remembered Gilda that morning, staring at her hand and mumbling something about a dress. 'That's what she was on about,' she said slowly. 'I saw her this morning. She obviously expected that I'd be wearing it, but I wasn't. I was crying over a list of pros and cons—well, pros, actually. There was only one con, and I don't think it applies.'

'What was it?' he asked.

She took a deep breath. 'I thought you'd hate me, after a while. I'd be in your house, untidying everything, the baby would be screaming, you'd be tired and fed up with us all, and I thought you'd start to wonder why on earth you'd agreed to it. But maybe you won't.'

'Not a chance,' he said, taking her hand and slipping the ring onto her finger. It was a perfect fit, a tiny bit on the loose side if anything, but that was probably as well as she was pregnant and her fingers might swell.

'You haven't actually asked me to marry you yet,' she reminded him. 'Not properly. Not for the right reasons.'

'I haven't? How remiss.'

He slid off the sofa onto his knees, took her hand in his and stared deep into her eyes. 'I love you, Cait,' he said carefully, every word clear so she couldn't possibly mistake it. 'I think I've loved you since I found you crying over your steering-wheel in the car park the day we took the kids to uni. I don't know if you love me. I hope you do, or that you'll learn to, because I know I'll love you till the day I die. Marry me, Cait. Let's be a family—a real family, all five of us. God knows, we all deserve it.'

Owen reached out a hand and brushed the tears

from her cheeks with his knuckles. 'Marry me, my darling. Please?'

She nodded, unable to speak, and then she swallowed hard and took a steadying breath. 'Of course I'll marry you—and of course I love you, you idiot!' she said, and then she was in his arms, wrapped hard against his chest, her mascara ruining the front of his beautiful cashmere sweater. 'Oh, look what I've done,' she said wretchedly when he straightened up.

'Forget it. You can cry all over everything I own for all I care. It's all yours anyway.' He pulled her to her feet, tutted and pushed her down again, then took off her ridiculous shoes. 'You can't walk in these, you'll mess your back up,' he said crossly, and lifted her into his arms.

'Where are you taking me?' she said curiously.

'Bed,' he replied. 'I'm tired. I want to lie down somewhere comfortable and hold you and listen to you telling me you love me until I fall asleep in your arms.'

'What a lovely idea. What about supper?'

'You want to eat, too?' he said, and put her down again. 'You're pregnant, aren't you, of course.'

She nodded.

'Pregnant women are always unreasonable. I should have remembered that.' He made a detour into the kitchen, picked up the biscuit tin and a bottle of mineral water and handed them to her, then scooped all of them up into his arms and carried her up to bed.

'You're looking very smug,' she remarked as he put her down in the middle of the bed.

'Am I?' Owen sat down beside her, his face suddenly serious. 'I don't mean to be. When Jill died, I thought I'd lost everything, and when Josh went away I felt as if I'd come to the end of the road. I was just thirty-nine, and there was nothing left for me except my career—

and then I met you. You've given me my life back, Cait. You've given me love and laughter, and another family to look forward to—a baby I thought I'd never have, a teenage daughter to test my patience and a beautiful woman to walk beside me through our lives. Can you blame me for looking just a tiny bit smug?'

His smile was gentle and a little sad, and she swallowed hard and hugged him.

'No. No, I can't. I feel the same.'

His eyes darkened and, taking the biscuits and the water away from her, he lay down beside her and took her into his arms. 'I love you,' he said softly, and kissed her…